Nicky Fifth's Five Alarm

by Lisa Funari-Willever

Franklin Mason Press
Columbus, New Jersey

For New Jersey's Bravest,
our career, volunteer, and forest firefighters
and for the families who support them and sacrifice
so much so they can protect everyone.

And to the children of New Jersey, may every choice
move you closer to your goals.

.

Franklin Mason Press ISBN: 978-1-7376768-0-5
Library of Congress Control Number: 2021944772
9 8 7 6 5 4 3 2

Cover Design by Monica Thomas, TLC Graphics
Printed and Published in the United States of America

Editorial Staff: Todd Willever, Jessica Willever, Patrick Willever, Tim Willever, Iris Hutchinson, Susan Willever, Paula Agabiti, Molly Agabiti, Maximus Agabiti, Marcia Jacobs, and Tiana Ristaino

www.franklinmasonpress.com
www.nickyfifth.com

Table of Contents

NICKY FIFTH'S
PASSPORT

NPF

Visit nickyfifth.com

Download and print your own free Nicky Fifth Passport. Use it whenever you visit the real NJ locations that the Nicky Fifth characters visit.

The Nicky Fifth Series

Book 1
32 Dandelion Court

Book 2
Garden State Adventure

Book 3
For Hire

Book 4
Passport to the Garden State

Book 5
At the Jersey Shore

Book 6
Nicky Fifth's New Jersey

Book 7
Nicky Fifth Says Vote For T-Bone

Book 8
Nicky Fifth Explores New Jersey's Great Outdoors

Book 9
T-Bone Takes a Stand For Public Schools

Book 10
Nicky Fifth Fit

Book 11
Nicky Fifth's Decisions, Decisions

Book 12
Nicky Fifth's Five Alarm

Chapter One

The Amazing, Magnificent Ernesto

"Nicky, wake up and come down," my mom yelled. "Tommy's here."

"Tell him to come back later," I hollered. "I'm asleep."

"You can't be asleep if you're talking," she replied.

"Okay," I said. "Then I'm trying to sleep."

"I really think you should come down here," she replied. "Now!"

When she added *now*, it meant start moving. It was one of those secret mom signals. *Now* at the end of a sentence, meant don't ask another question.

I rubbed my eyes and took a deep breath. The only predictable thing about my best friend, Tommy Rizzo, or T-Bone as he was known, was his unpredictability. My dad often described him as volatile. My mom insisted volatile was too negative. She called him spirited. My grandfather just called him a firecracker.

When I reached the bottom step, I caught a glimpse of him. My mom wasn't overreacting when she said to come down now.

"Good morning, Nicholas," he said, bending slightly and then tipping a top hat.

I looked at my mom and she shrugged. T-Bone was wearing a tuxedo with tails, a top hat, and white gloves. He was holding a very awkward pose, apparently waiting for a compliment. I scrambled to think of something nice to say. He looked so familiar, like something I had seen before. Then it hit me. "You look like you escaped from the top of a wedding cake." I wasn't sure if that qualified as nice.

"Well, I think you look very dapper," said my mom. "By any chance, are you going to a wedding?"

"Or getting married?" I added, trying not to laugh.

"Maybe this will help," he said as he reached back and pulled part of a black cape with red lining over his shoulder.

Before we could speak, my dad walked in, saw T-Bone, abruptly stopped, and returned to the kitchen.

"What are you wearing?" I asked.

"Look," he said as he pointed over his shoulder to the three giant, glittery words embroidered on the cape, *The Amazing Ernesto.*

"What does that even mean?" I asked. "Who's Ernesto?"

"I am," he replied.

"No, you're T-Bone," I said like I was talking to an amnesia patient. "Your name is Tommy Rizzo, but we call you T-Bone. Say, did you hit your head or something?"

"Obviously, my real name is Tommy Rizzo. I know that, Nick," he said. "This is my amazing new stage name. I am *The Great Ernesto.*"

"Are you sure, because your cape says *The Amazing Ernesto,*" I pointed out.

"Ah," he sighed, "I am *The Great Amazing Ernesto* and I am at your service. Your wish is my command."

"Nope, according to your poncho, you're just *The Amazing Ernesto,*" I corrected.

"Ok," he sighed as he tried reading the cape upside down, "I am *The Amazing Ernesto* and I am at your service. Your wish is my command."

"Honey, what a great idea to hire a butler," said my father. "I always wanted a butler. So, what do I want? Oh, wait, I've got it. Tommy, I'll take a black coffee and a cheese danish."

T-Bone looked confused. "I'm not a butler, Mr. A. I don't even know how to buttle. I don't even know the recipe for coffee."

"Well, that's disappointing," my dad said with a grin. "But it does beg the question, what are you supposed to be?"

"I'm *The Attractive Ernesto*," he answered, once again flipping the cape forward and pointing. "It says so right here."

"Amazing," I repeated.

"Either way," said T-Bone.

"Okay, better question," I interrupted. "Who is *The Amazing Ernesto*? And does he know you have his stuff?"

"How about an even better question? Did you see our summer assignment? We have to decide what we want to be when we grow up," a suddenly flustered T-Bone explained. "And I have no idea what to pick, so I decided to just go into the family business and be a magician."

"A magician?" my mom and I said at the same time. "Family business?"

"This was my great-grandfather's uniform," T-Bone exclaimed with pride.

"You mean his costume?" asked my mother.

"Nope, a costume is for people pretending to be something," he explained. "My great-grandfather was a real magician. He was actually magical. And since it was his job, this is a uniform."

"Wait, your *great*-grandfather, Ernesto, was a magician?" I asked.

"Nope," he replied. "My great-grandfather was Joe the barber."

"I thought you said…" I began before I was interrupted.

"My great-grandfather, Joe, was a barber," he explained. "When his favorite customer died, he left my grandfather this uniform."

"Then what?" I asked.

"Obviously, my grandfather immediately quit his job and became a magician," he said.

"Obviously," said my dad.

"And you're wearing it because?" I asked, waiting for him to fill in the blank.

"Well, I need to test drive my new career," he began. "But I also want to stand out in high school. You know, I want to be known. I want to be seen."

"Well, if you wear that get up, you'll be known and seen alright," my dad said as he shook his head and laughed.

"Exactly," said T-Bone. "I'll be known as the *Magnificent Ernesto.*"

"Amazing," I corrected him, once again. "It's amazing."

"I know, right?" he nodded. "This is definitely amazing."

"No, your poncho says *The Amazing Ernesto*," I said. "Why can't you remember that one word? And, also, you cannot, under any circumstances, wear that outfit to high school. Ever."

"Nick, it's a cape, not a poncho," he corrected. "But, I hear what you're saying. It's too big. I was afraid the size might be a big problem. It's a little roomy on me because my great-grandfather loved the ravioli. Should I see a tailor so I don't look silly?"

"So, when you looked in the mirror, the only problem you saw was the size?" asked my dad. "That is just fascinating. Utterly fascinating."

"What's your opinion, Mr. A.," asked T-Bone. "How should I approach high school?"

"Try being normal," my dad replied as he returned to the kitchen.

"What my husband means," said my mom, "is that freshman year of high school is when you meet so many new people and you might just want to go in a little less flashy. Plus, this magic thing may just be a phase. You don't want to be known as *the magician* and end up not really liking magic, right?"

Unlike my dad, my mom worked overtime to avoid hurting anyone's feelings. And, while she made some good points, I wasn't sure that her logic would get through to T-Bone.

"That's a good point," he said. "I should practice my magic to see if this will be my lifelong passion and reason for living."

"Lifelong passion and reason for living?" asked my mom. "That's a lot to ask of your great-grandfather's costume."

"Oh, it's a uniform, Mrs. A., but I see what you're saying," he conceded. "So, you think I should practice some magic before I commit to a lifelong career or hobby?"

"That's probably a good idea," she agreed. "Why don't you show us some of your tricks?"

T-Bone froze. This was the exact moment he realized he didn't know any magic tricks.

"Yeah, Ernie, maybe pull a rabbit out of that giant top hat," I suggested. "You know, since you're a real, amazing magician."

T-Bone raised a hand, indicating that he would like silence. Then he pulled the cape over his arm and covered his face. He took several deep breaths and said, "Ladies and gentlemen, *The Amazing Ernesto* will now perform his newest trick. Please lower your heads, close your eyes, and count to six."

"Six?" I asked.

"Yeah, the magic number is now six," he hastily confirmed. "Three had a good run, but now we're going with six."

"Why six?" I asked. "Why not the more popular five or ten? Or the very lucky seven?"

"Because the new number is six," he said, "as in a half dozen or the bottom number on a clock. Now, please, count to six."

My mom and I shrugged and did as he instructed. By the time we reached four, we heard a loud bang. We opened our eyes and started laughing. The banging was the sound of our front door slamming shut. Using those extra seconds to make a very quick escape would probably be his best trick.

My dad returned and asked, "Who was at the door?"

"No one," my mom laughed. "It turns out the only trick Tommy knows is how to disappear. We closed our eyes and he ran right out. When we opened our eyes, he was gone."

"You mean after all these years of Tommy practically living here and eating all of our food, all I had to do was ask him to do a magic trick and he would've disappeared? Just like that?" my dad said as he shook his head.

"Seems like it," my mom said with a shrug. "Nick, maybe you should call him and see if he's okay."

"Or," I suggested, "maybe I can go back to sleep and assume he's working on a new, more amazing magic trick."

I returned to my room, ready to go back to sleep and unsee what I had just seen. Unfortunately, T-Bone had gotten into my head. He made me start thinking about my own future and career. I started to stress over how little thought I had given high school. My whole plan was to just show up on the first day. That was it, the whole plan: just show up. I never thought I needed a hobby, or considered wearing a glittery embroidered cape. Just thinking about it all exhausted me right back to sleep. If only that sleep could have lasted more than twelve minutes.

"Nick, Houdini's back," my dad yelled up to my room.

How could he possibly be back already? I had just closed my eyes. I needed to find a polite way to ask him to leave.

"Tell him to do that trick again," I replied, hoping this sounded like something a supportive friend would say.

My mom calmly hollered one word up the stairs, "Now!"

When I returned to the family room, T-Bone was no longer wearing the top hat and tails. This time he was now wearing a colonial costume.

"So, Nick, did you give any thought to what you want to be when you grow up?" he asked as if nothing was different. "You don't want to wait until the last minute. And honestly, you should test drive everything you think you might want to do."

"Sorry, Paul Revere," I said, "I was trying to sleep. Thanks for sounding the alarm. Now, once again, good night."

"What's with the outfit?" asked my dad. "Did you get a job at the Old Barracks Museum?"

"If only," he said with a shrug. "Working at the Old Barracks Museum would be awesome. Working side by side with Richard, Asher, and the gang would be amazing. But no, I was taking a new, or should I say *old*, identity for a test drive. I'm considering being a history buff. What do you think, Mr. A.?"

"As your career?" asked my dad, visibly confused.

"Sure," answered T-Bone. "Why not?"

"First," my dad began, "history buff isn't an actual career. Second, when someone is a buff it means that's what they're interested in, like a hobby. And finally, aren't you hot wearing wool on a humid summer day?"

"Fair point," said T-Bone. "So I'll become a professional buff. Or is it a buffet? Or a buffer? Or a bufferino?"

"Okay, not only are none of those words actual jobs," I began, "one is part of a car wash and the other is an all you can eat restaurant."

"Sorry, Nick," said T-Bone, "but I think I'll defer to your dad's judgment. This requires the advice of someone who's worked for years, toiling, sweating, and driving a tractor in the hot sun."

"You do realize I'm the produce manager of a grocery store, right?" asked my dad.

"Exactly," said T-Bone. "You're out there planting and picking, packing and shipping, grinding every day."

"You have no idea what I do, do you?" asked my dad.

"Sure, I do," said T-Bone. "You're the produce manager. You manage all the fruits and vegetables from start to finish. From wee baby seedlings to delicious casseroles."

"Tommy, I don't plant, grow, or manage produce. I manage the produce department in a grocery store. The farmers, suppliers, picker/packers, and drivers get the fruits and vegetables to my store and then I manage that department. I'm the last stop in the food chain. And I definitely don't make casseroles."

"Too bad, because that's not nearly as glamorous as I imagined," T-Bone shrugged. "Although that does explain why you don't wear jeans and workboots to work and why you work during the winter and on rainy days."

"Well, there's also the minor detail that I live in a suburban neighborhood," my dad continued. "Where did you think I was doing all of this toiling, sweating, and farming?"

"Good point," agreed T-Bone. "I assumed the store where you work had a big farm nearby. My other possible explanation was that you were a master hydroponic gardener."

"A master hydroponic gardener?" my dad gasped.

"You're not familiar with the term?" T-Bone asked. "It's a way to grow fruits, vegetables, and even flowers without dirt. They use lights and water. You should check it out."

"I'm very familiar with hydroponic gardening," said my dad. "It can solve food shortages for countries with difficult growing conditions and make fresh fruits and vegetables a reality for people who live in urban and impoverished areas. But, just out of curiosity and because you're here every day, don't you think you would have known if I was a hydroponic gardener?"

"You mean Master Hydroponic Gardener," T-Bone corrected. "Another fair point. But, since you do have an actual job, I'm gonna take your advice, anyway. So, which way should I go?"

"If you insist," said my dad. "I only have one question - does this colonial character do that six-second disappearing trick?"

"No way, Mr. A.," said T-Bone, "that trick is reserved for official magicians only."

"Then I have made my decision and wholeheartedly vote for the magician," said my dad.

Chapter Two

I'll Have What Joe Had

Compared to how it started, the rest of the day was actually pretty normal. This time when I tried to go back to sleep, it worked. Unfortunately, it worked a little too well. By the time I woke up, it was way past lunch. I headed to the kitchen and spotted a note on the counter. *Went to the store, be back soon. Don't eat too much, we're going out for dinner.*

As I plopped on the couch, I noticed just how quiet the house could be. Between my parents, my brother, Timmy, my sisters, Maggie and Emma, and my friends, T-Bone and Wanda, our house was never quiet. While they didn't live here, they might as well have, as they were here every day.

I headed to the kitchen to grab a handful of pretzels, not sure what *don't eat too much* really meant. A moment later, the front door opened, followed by quick footsteps. Naturally, I assumed it was T-Bone and yelled, "I'm in the kitchen weirdo."

"Okay, dork," said my grandfather.

"Oh, sorry, Pop," I said, "I thought you were T-Bone."

"I figured that," he laughed.

"I didn't know you were coming over," I said. "No one's here right now."

"I know," he replied, "I'm early."

"Early for what?" I asked.

"For dinner," he said.

He explained that my grandmother was going to Bingo with a neighbor and he thought it would be fun to visit one of his favorite restaurants. It was called Rossi's Bar & Grill and he said it first became famous on Franklin Street in Trenton. When I asked him why it was so famous, he said it was because they served the most incredible burgers. People came from all over to try a Rossi Burger. When I asked him if any famous people came to eat the famous burgers, he mentioned lots of names, but the one that really grabbed my attention was Joe DiMaggio. I couldn't believe I would be eating in the exact same place where Yankee Great Joltin' Joe ate. That's when my grandfather informed me that they moved to Hamilton, but I'd still get to meet the owner, Mike Rossi.

"Did he play on the Yankees?" I asked. Even though I was a die-hard Phillies fan, I had total respect for all MLB players.

"Actually, Mike was a great ballplayer," said Pop. "He played baseball and football at Rutgers University, but was sidelined by an injury. And his dad, Alfie, played professional baseball. Both were good friends with Joe DiMaggio and Mickey Mantle."

"Joe D and The Mick? Two amazing hall-of-famers?" I gasped. "I have one question, why are we still standing here? Can we go now?"

"We could," said Pop, "but I thought you'd like to wait for your family, as well as T-Bone, and Wanda."

Not only did Pop invite my family, he also invited T-Bone and Wanda. Luckily, T-Bone opted not to wear a costume, or a uniform. While I went in Pop's car with my friends, the rest of my family piled into my mom's van. Before we knew it, we were turning into the driveway and could smell the burgers from the parking lot. Hopefully, Mike Rossi was working tonight.

Since there were nine of us, we sat at a long table in the back. There was a floor-to-ceiling curtain hanging that was filled with giant black and white pictures of the original location on Franklin Street. As soon as we sat down, a man came over and said, "It's about time you brought the family."

"Mike, you look great," Pop said, followed by a hug and a handshake. "The wife sends her regards, but she's playing Bingo. You know how it is."

"I do. Tell her we missed seeing her," Mike nodded and turned to my dad, "Wait, this can't be your son, little Jimmy?"

"Little Jimmy!" T-Bone blurted out and started laughing. My dad shot him a look.

"Hi, Mike," said my dad as he stood up to shake his hand. "It's really nice to see you again."

"Wow," Mike said as he scanned the table. "No wonder I haven't seen you in years. Six kids must keep you pretty busy."

My dad almost spit out his water. He introduced my mom and my family and then explained that Wanda and T-Bone weren't *his* kids, but *my* friends.

"Well, I hope you're all hungry," said Mike. "Jessica will take great care of you. I'll be back in a bit."

The menu looked amazing, but I didn't need it. I was getting whatever Joe Di Maggio ordered, unless he didn't order the burger. Hopefully, he ordered the burger.

While I was admiring the pictures hung all over the walls, our server came over. "Hi, my name is Jessica, and I'll be taking care of you this evening."

"Excuse me," T-Bone interrupted, "are you one of the original servers and did you ever serve Joe DiMaggio? And if you did, did he order the Rossi Burger? It will help my friend, Nick, make up his mind."

She looked stunned. She was probably only twenty-one years old and was shocked by the question. Luckily, Pop stepped in. "Tommy, I'm sure that's a question for Mike. Sorry, Jessica, math isn't his best subject."

"Same here," said Jessica with a smile.

I held my breath, hoping T-Bone didn't offend her. Luckily, she laughed and said, "I wasn't even born when Joe DiMaggio was alive. Maybe I need to try a new moisturizer."

"Nope, your moisturizer isn't the problem," my mom said while shaking her head and looking at T-Bone.

"It's all good," Jessica laughed, "I have a couple of brothers. In fact, my brother, Patrick, will be bringing out your food tonight. And before you ask, he's a year younger than me, so no, he didn't meet Joe DiMaggio either."

"How about your other brother?" asked T-Bone. "Perhaps he crossed paths with Joltin' Joe?"

"Timmy?" she laughed. "He's the youngest, so they definitely didn't cross paths.

"I'm the youngest brother, too," my brother said as he lurched forward, "and my name is Timmy."

"Another Timmy?" Patrick said as he dropped off our waters.

"Another one," Jess said with a smile.

While we smoothed everything over with our server, Mike returned with Alan Meinster, his business partner. They began telling my favorite kind of stories: *good-old-days stories.* We had learned about prohibition during our history class and now we were learning that the original Rossi's started as a candy store in the front and a speakeasy in the back. Incredible, I thought. It's often so hard to imagine the world before you're born. Then, you meet someone like Mike who actually lived many of the things you learn about. His stories were fascinating, funny, and so detailed. It was as though he closed his eyes and was transported right back to the time he was describing. And, when he spoke about his grandparents and parents, you could just feel the pride. Mike clearly was a natural storyteller.

"Did your grandfather start the restaurant all by himself?" asked Wanda.

"It was my grandfather, Mike, my grandmother, Anna, and my Aunt Pearl. Then came my dad, Alfie, and his brother, Gil. Then most of the grandkids like me, my sister, Sharon, my brother Jimmy, and my cousin, Chip, got involved. We're all third generation, and do you see that server over there?" he said as he pointed. "That's my daughter, Joanna. She's Mike and Anna's great-granddaughter, making her the fourth generation."

"Wow, four generations," said my mom. "What a legacy."

"Any of you kids interested in becoming a chef?" asked Mike.

"Recently, I've been thinking about my future," said T-Bone. "We have one of those 'what do you want to be when you grow up' summer assignments, so I've been trying to narrow down my choices."

"What are you stuck between?" asked Alan.

"I was between magician and history buff," T-Bone began.

"Is history buff a job?" asked Mike.

"It is if you have a uniform," said T-Bone. "And I have a pretty cool uniform. But on the ride over here, I changed my mind. Now, I'm somewhere between astronaut and deep-sea diver."

"Deep sea diver?" asked Alan. "That's different. Don't most kids want to be firefighters or something like that."

"I'm looking for something that's actually a little dangerous," said T-Bone, totally dismissing the firefighter idea. "Imagine floating around the moon or diving like 20 feet."

Mike laughed and said, "I've done some diving myself and deep-sea diving goes a little deeper than 20 feet. And sure, being an astronaut is definitely pretty high on the danger scale, but so is being a firefighter."

"Not really," T-Bone said as if he knew what he was talking about.

"Not really?" Mike asked. "Are you saying firefighting isn't a dangerous job?"

"That's exactly what I'm saying," T-Bone confirmed. "I think Hollywood makes it look crazy dangerous for movie ticket sales. Most days they probably sleep or get kittens out of trees."

Everyone was speechless. We were completely and literally speechless.

"You might not want to say that too loud," warned Alan. "The table next to you is a group of firefighters."

"Which table?" asked T-Bone as he started to stand.

Before my mom could stop him, he was already introducing himself to the next table.

"Excuse me, are you firefighters?" he asked.

"That depends," said one of the men. "Who wants to know?"

"Just me," T-Bone responded. "I have a question for you. You see, me and my friends, Wanda and Nicky over there, are New Jersey's Unofficial Junior Ambassadors. We visit places all over the state and report on them. Then we give our reports to the Governor's Office. It's a good gig even though they haven't made us official yet and we'll probably never get paid. But we do get to see the entire state and meet a lot of great people."

Oh boy, T-Bone was rambling.

"That's nice," said another very confused man. "Was there a question in there?"

"Actually, yes," said T-Bone, "as we've explored New Jersey, we've met a lot of great firefighters. They were all really good people and we even worked on literacy programs with them. Have you ever heard of Code Read in the City of Trenton?"

"I sure have," said the first firefighter. "And we've met before. My name is Wayne Wolk and I'm from the Trenton Fire Department. We helped you deliver books to every elementary school student in the City of Trenton. Was that your question?"

"No, I'm getting there," said T-Bone. "So, my question is about the danger level of your occupation. On a scale of 0-100, how would you rate firefighting?"

Everyone at our table was holding their breath. We were all terrified that he was about to insult some of New Jersey's bravest. As it turned out, we had every reason to be nervous.

"I'll tell you what," said another firefighter, "My name is Eddie Donnelly. I'm a Union Township Firefighter and the president of the New Jersey State Firefighters Mutual Benevolent Association. Before we answer your question, I'd love to hear what you think."

"Wow, I don't know what a Mutual Fire Gelatin Association is," T-Bone began answering, "but it sounds delicious."

They all laughed. "It's not gelatin, it's benevolent," said Eddie. "We're the labor organization that works to protect firefighters. So, how would you rate our occupation for danger?"

"A solid 40," he proclaimed with a nod. "And I'm sure you'll agree that I'm being very generous."

While T-Bone appeared proud of himself, we were horrified. It was the equivalent of rating Joe DiMaggio or Mickey Mantle as average ballplayers. How could anyone rate firefighters a 40 on the 0-100 danger scale.

"A solid 40?" asked Wayne. "Mind if I ask how you arrived at that number?"

"Well, you see, I figured, like most people, you guys work like 8 hours in a row," said T-Bone. "During that time, you have to subtract for meals, television, cooking, walking the dalmatians, naps, bagpiping, parades, and cleaning the trucks. None of those activities is even a 20 on the danger scale. If you throw in the sporadic kitten up a tree and random fire alarm, it gets you to, maybe, a 30. An occasional fire brings you to a solid 40. It's Hollywood that makes firefighting seem so dangerous."

"Is that a fact?" asked Eddie.

"Wow, you seem pretty confident about a day in the life of a firefighter," said Wayne. "But, you did get a few things wrong."

"For starters, most of us work 24-hours," a firefighter named Tim Duetsch corrected him. "That's 24-hours in a row."

"Really?" asked T-Bone. "Are you sure, because that would be a whole day and that seems like a bit much."

"Positive," said Tim.

"Then the real question is," T-Bone continued. "How many hours do you actually have to be awake?"

They looked at each other and laughed. "Most shifts, almost all of them. We sleep around 11:00 pm, but get up all night long."

"All night long?" wondered T-Bone. "Bad dreams? Try cutting back on spicy food and scary movies right before bed."

"We aren't getting up for bad dreams," Wayne laughed. "We're getting up all night to respond to calls."

"Have you tried turning off the ringer?" asked T-Bone.

"Not phone calls," said Wayne. "These are emergency calls."

"I see," said T-Bone. "But what if the fire bell rings after you've gone to sleep? Do they send the nighttime crew out so you can continue to sleep?"

"We are the nighttime crew," they all replied.

"So, you mean to tell me that if you're sound asleep and the bell rings, you have to get up, get dressed, and get ready to fight a fire in what, like less than an hour?"

The laughter got louder. "So, we arrive, ready to respond to any emergency, in roughly 3 minutes. And for a reference, the national average is 3-4 minutes," said Eddie.

"Wait, three minutes? It takes me longer than that to start my morning stretches," said T-Bone. "I hope you don't run out before you properly stretch? That could be super dangerous."

"Emergencies don't wait for First Responders to properly stretch," said Wayne, using air quotes for the words properly stretch. "And, to save time, we leave our boots inside our bunker pants, right next to where we sit in the truck."

"Hey, that's clever," T-Bone nodded. "But you really should think about building some time into your emergency schedule for proper stretching."

"Yeah, so we don't actually schedule our emergencies," said Wayne, bringing out the air quotes again for the word *schedule.*

"See, there you go," T-Bone continued, "maybe you should consider creating an emergency schedule."

At that moment, I noticed my parents and my grandfather had all lowered their heads and sighed.

"I have a good idea," said Eddie. "But, first, who does this kid belong to?"

Everyone continued to look down, even my mom. After what seemed like an unusually long and uncomfortable silence, I finally claimed him. "He's my friend."

"Okay, Nicky," said Eddie, "I have an idea. Why don't I arrange for you and your friends to visit some New Jersey firehouses to get a, let's just say, more realistic perspective of what firefighting is really like? Since you're junior tour guides, maybe you could share what the state's firefighters do. This conversation convinced me that we really need to work on our messaging."

"Two things," said T-Bone. "First, we're Unofficial Junior Ambassadors, not tour guides. And second, are we talking about a ride along? Like on TV?"

"Let's refer to this as an eye opener," Eddie said with a smile.

"Consider it like a social studies lesson," said Wayne. "You'll be learning about community helpers."

"Or like career day," Tim added.

"I'll call a couple of departments and arrange for you to visit," said Eddie. "Then, if you still have questions, I can answer them for you."

A few minutes later, T-Bone had returned to his seat with their contact information and the firefighters left. I didn't have proof, but I was pretty sure they decided to leave before T-Bone could return.

When Patrick delivered our food, we were speechless. The Rossi Burger was huge and even better than I expected. Mike told us how they became so enormous. It turned out that his dad, Alfie, was so big he could hold five baseballs in one hand. Since Alfie always made the burgers, it was no wonder they were almost as big as my sister's head.

I tried to finish my burger, but eventually surrendered and asked for a box. Except for my dad, we all took half home. Just when I thought I couldn't eat another bite, Jessica and Joanna passed out dishes of peanut butter ice cream.

"Thanks," said my grandfather, winking at Mike. "We can't have them leaving Rossi's without the ice cream, can we?"

"No, we can't," Mike agreed. "No, we can't."

Chapter Three

I'll Sell You A Slice

The next day, when Wanda came over, she seemed pretty excited. She told me she had just finished, *some light research.* What she called *light*, was really college thesis-level research.

"Nick, I was thinking about our dinner last night," she said as she rifled through her messenger bag.

"Yeah, that burger was amazing," I replied. "I can't decide if I want the other half for breakfast, lunch, or dinner."

"It was definitely amazing," she agreed. "But I was referring to T-Bone's conversation with the firefighters."

"That was pretty ridiculous," I nodded. "It makes you wonder where he gets his information."

"Exactly," said Wanda. "That's my point. T-Bone does have a lot of misinformation."

"So, what are you thinking?" I asked, knowing she probably already had a plan.

"T-Bone can't be the only person who doesn't know what first responders do," she explained. "And if we share the factual information we're about to learn, people will be safer and reduce the number of emergencies they need to respond to."

"You got my attention," I said. "What do we need to do?"

"I think we take Eddie up on his offer to visit some firehouses. We can ask the firefighters what peole can do to stay safe which will help keep them safe," she said.

"Who are we keeping safe?" T-Bone asked as he walked in and sat down. "The polar bears? Bald eagles? Honeybees? Even though I love nature, it gets a high score on the danger scale. You really do have to keep your guard up."

"All good causes," I agreed. "But I think Wanda was talking about firefighters and regular people."

"Interesting," T-Bone replied. "But if you're talking about every person who is a firefighter and then every person who isn't a firefighter, isn't that everybody?"

"He's not wrong," said Wanda. "So that makes this even more important. This affects everyone."

"What should we do?" I asked, confident that Wanda would have the best solution.

"That's easy," said T-Bone. "We visit every firehouse at least once, possibly twice. We ask them questions, write down their answers, and then write a report about it. Easy greasy."

"You mean easy peasy," said Wanda. "It's easy peasy."

"Nope, I'm quite sure it's *easy greasy*," T-Bone corrected.

"That doesn't even make any sense," I said.

"Of course, it does," T-Bone began to explain. "When something is squeaking or tight, what do carpenters and mechanics do? They grease it. When your mom is cooking eggs and she doesn't want them to stick to the pan, what does she do? She greases it. Grease is good. And what's a *peasy*, anyway?"

I knew he was wrong, but his easy greasy explanation made so much sense, we didn't argue with him. We did, however, have several problems with his plan to visit every firehouse. For starters, it would take all day just to visit the firehouses in Trenton and according to Wanda, there were hundreds of firehouses in New Jersey. There was no way we could visit every firehouse once, let alone twice. And another problem would be that the information would most likely be similar coming from firehouses in the same area.

"T-Bone, do you have any idea how long that would take?" asked Wanda.

"A good day, or two," he said, proving he really had no idea. "And besides the visits, we should buy some firefighter costumes and maybe adopt our own dalmatian. What could possibly gain the respect of real firefighters more than dressing like firefighters and walking in with a dalmatian?"

"Why stop at one dalmatian?" Wanda asked sarcastically. "Why not get a dozen? Or better yet, 101 dalmatians?"

"I know you're excited," T-Bone replied, "but 101 dalmatians would be a lot of work. Plus, where would we keep them?"

Wanda looked like she was about to scream. It was time to intervene.

"T-Bone, we're not visiting every firehouse, we're not buying uniforms, and we're definitely not adopting dogs" I said. "As far as ideas go, this is definitely not your best."

"Everyone's a critic," he said, shrugging his shoulders.

"I think we should call Eddie and follow his suggestion," I began. "Let's visit a few firehouses from different areas, talk to some firefighters, and do a safety report."

"We should also find out about careers in the fire service," said Wanda.

"Don't forget the chili," said T-Bone. "We can judge the chili when we get to each house."

"What chili?" I asked.

"C'mon guys, they're firefighters," said T-Bone. "You don't think every shift has a prize-winning batch of chili on the stove?"

"You do?" I asked.

"Of course," T-Bone nodded. "Unless it's one of their pose-for-a-calendar days."

"Pose-for-a-calendar days?" Wanda shrieked.

"Of course, they pose for calendars," T-Bone insisted. "I'm telling you; this is a very Hollywood career."

"You're gonna be shocked when you see what firefighters really do," I said. "You know, a firehouse isn't a Hollywood set filled with lights and cameras."

"Unless, of course, it's pose-for-a-calendar day," T-Bone added with a shrug.

Rather than listen to T-Bone's theories on the fire service, we decided to call Eddie and set up our visits. The sooner we could spend time with firefighters across the state the sooner we could dispel the myths T-Bone had created. Unfortunately, he wasn't available, and we had to leave a message.

"He's probably at a photo shoot," said T-Bone.

"Hey guys," my dad said as he entered the room. "I have to take a ride to Robbinsville and I was thinking of stopping at DeLorenzo's. Anybody want to…"

Before he could finish his sentence, we all jumped up and said yes. It had been way too long since we had the most amazing tomato pie on the planet. Thirty minutes later, we were walking in the front door.

"Look who it is," said Sam, the tomato pie genius owner. "My favorite Junior Ambassadors."

"I'm pretty sure we're the only Junior Ambassadors you know," I said.

"Hey, they can both be true," Sam said with a smile. "You're the only ambassadors I know *and* you're my favorites."

"That sir, is an excellent point," said T-Bone.

"Give us about 20-25 minutes for a table to open up," said Sam.

"It's always worth the wait," said my dad as we headed for the waiting area. Less than a minute after we sat down, T-Bone found himself in a conversation with a group of ladies. He definitely had an approachable face.

"If you're really hungry, I'll sell you a slice," said the older woman.

"I'm starving," said T-Bone. "How much?"

"She's joking," I whispered.

"How do you know?" he whispered back.

"Because she was laughing when she said it and also, how could she sell you a slice?" I whispered, wondering why he had such a hard time with jokes. "Why would she wait for a table if she had slices to sell?"

"Interesting," T-Bone said, pointing to the woman's Titanic replica purse. "I'm a huge fan of the Titanic."

"Thank you," she said. "Me, too. I just love history, so I had to have it."

"It's a shame they didn't give it lights and a foghorn, though?" he said as he examined it closer. "They didn't, did they?"

"It's a purse, dear," the woman said, "not a toy truck."

"So, do you come here often?" T-Bone inquired. "We're New Jersey's *still* Unofficial Junior Ambassadors and we found DeLorenzo's years ago. I'm T-Bone."

She smiled and said, "Well hello, T-Bone, my name is Rosie Kostival and I'm very happy to meet you. This is my daughter, Denise, my daughter, Debbie, and our friend, Peggy. And yes, we come here very often."

"Did you know the original DeLorenzo's was on Hudson Street in Trenton?" he asked.

"I sure did," she said with a smile. "Did you know I used to live on Bayard Street in Trenton?"

"I didn't," said T-Bone as he scratched his head. "How did I not know that?"

"Probably because we just met," she guessed.

"Good point," he agreed. "I love coming here, but I wish we didn't have to wait for a table."

"You're looking at it all wrong, dear," she said, still smiling. "Right now, as you're waiting for your table, you're smelling that warm tomato pie and watching as pies get delivered to other tables. You're imagining what that first bite will taste like. I try to enjoy the wait."

"Enjoy the wait?" T-Bone gasped.

"When you get to be my age, you'll find that it's wise to enjoy everything," she laughed, "even waiting for a table."

"Wow, that's a great attitude," T-Bone conceded. "How old are you?"

"Why don't you guess?" she suggested.

"No way," he said. "I always lose this game. I once told my 45-year-old teacher that there was a senior citizen discount at the grocery store and she was not happy about that."

"Go ahead," she said. "I promise not to get upset."

"Do you want to tell me who was president when you were born?" asked T-Bone.

"Nope," she laughed.

"Okay," he said, scratching his head. "I'm gonna go with, um, probably, er, this is really not a good idea."

"I'll give you a hint," she said. "I was born in the middle of the Great Depression, before freezers were in homes, while Herbert Hoover was the president, and Lou Gherig and Babe Ruth were crushing it."

"Yikes, are you 120-years-old?" T-Bone gasped, covering his mouth. "Because, if you are, you look amazing!"

"Wow, you really aren't good at this game, are you?" she said.

"Older?" he asked.

Thankfully, Rosie was a great sport and in T-Bone's defense, he did warn her. When she told us she was 90-years-old, we were all shocked. She was a petite person, like my grandmother, with short white hair. I didn't know many 90-year-olds, or any, for that matter, but she sure seemed younger. She was very stylish, wore make-up, and even carried a Titanic purse.

"Are you really 90-years-old?" asked Wanda. "You look so much younger."

"Nope," she answered. "I'm *90-years-young.* Age really is just a number."

"How do you do it? How do you stay so young?" asked Wanda. "What's your secret?"

"I laugh every day," she said. "I love mingling with people and learning about them. I also love fashion and anything that can make you feel good."

"I think most 90-year-olds wear old lady dresses," said T-Bone. "Aren't you kinda out of uniform?"

"Oh, I've always been ahead of my time when it comes to fashion and design," she explained. "I think people should wear what makes them happy. I'm happy being fashionable."

"Do you have any other advice?" asked Wanda.

"I have plenty, but since my table is ready, I'll leave you with this," she began, "family, good friends, and good food. If you surround yourself with those things, you'll live a happy life."

It must have been true. She was happy, active, and strong. When we were called to our table, we decided to add her in our next report. New Jersey's kids could always use great examples and words of wisdom. Clearly, Rosie offered both. We all agreed that she was a New Jersey treasure.

One hour and four pies later, we waved the white flag. Despite our best efforts, we couldn't eat another super thin slice. While everyone was talking, I noticed a very distracted T-Bone staring at the people seated right behind us.

"Nick, Nick, that guy is from the Capital City Community Coalition," said T-Bone, vigorously tilting his head. "Do you remember, him? He's friends with Pastor Taylor. Don't look."

"I don't know," I said as I started to turn around to take a look. "I'd have to see him to know."

"No, don't turn around," he said very firmly.

"Then how can I see if I recognize him?" I asked.

"Good point," he said. "Just be slick when you turn around."

I slowly turned my head and realized T-Bone was right. I couldn't remember his name, but he was from the Attorney General's office. I also knew that, given T-Bone's level of excitement, we'd know for sure in about five seconds.

"Hi, I don't know if you remember me," T-Bone began as he approached them, "my name is Tommy Rizzo and me and my friends met you at the Capital City Community Coalition."

"Of course, I recognize you," the man said.

"Was it my rugged good looks?" T-Bone asked with a big smile.

"Sure," he said, "and the fact that you're significantly younger than most members of our coalition. Anyway, I'm Dave

Leonardis, from the Attorney General's Office and this is Dr. Mark McLaughlin, from St. Francis Medical Center."

"Oh, we go way back with Attorney General Gurbir Grewal," said T-Bone. "And Mercer County Prosecutor Angelo Onofri. We get to meet a lot of important people."

"If I recall, you spoke to General Grewal about drug abuse and opioids, correct?" asked Dave.

"Correct," said T-Bone.

"That's impressive," said Dr. McLaughlin. "It's nice to see kids get involved in serious issues."

"We cover everything," said T-Bone. "A lot of kids read our reports, so we try to mix it up. We've covered poverty, civics, the environment, businesses, wellness, and even drug abuse."

"So, what are you working on now?" asked Dave.

"Funny you should ask," said T-Bone. "We're working on some fire safety issues and fire stuff with some firefighters at some firehouses. Not all of them. Just a few firehouses and some firefighters to talk about fire stuff and fire safety."

"Well, you sound all *fired up*," said Dr. McLaughlin with a laugh.

"What do you mean?" asked T-Bone, clearly not getting the doctor's joke.

"Never mind," said Dr. McLaughlin. "But since you're junior ambassadors, I'm thinking we should give you our Beat The Streets flyer."

He handed T-Bone a flyer and T-Bone looked confused. "Are you inviting me to be a street boxer, because I'm more of a lover than a fighter."

Dave and Dr. McLaughlin both laughed. "No, not at all. This is the Trenton Youth Wrestling Beat The Streets program for kids. We have a clinic coming up at Rivera School in Trenton. You should come by and check it out."

"Do I have to wrestle?" asked T-Bone. "Because I'm more of a…"

"Yes, a lover, not a fighter. We got it," Dave interrupted. "Don't worry, our wrestlers have extensive training. Many are elite athletes. We would never ask our spectators to wrestle."

"Will we be in danger of having a chair thrown at us?" T-Bone inquired. "Will we be seated in the splash zone?"

"This isn't TV wrestling or an aquatic show," Dave said with a laugh. "This is the real thing, and our kids are doing quite well."

"Then we'll definitely check it out," said T-Bone.

With business cards in hand, he returned to our table to share the conversation. Leave it to T-Bone to recognize everyone he's ever met. Luckily, it didn't look like he bothered them too much and the wrestling sounded pretty interesting.

"I'm starting to feel like T-Bone is the Mayor of DeLorenzo's," said my dad. "Is there anyone else he'll need to speak with before we leave?"

My mom looked around and laughed. "There are about 12 tables between here and the door, so I'd say the chances are fairly good that he'll see someone else he knows."

"Or meet someone new," added Wanda. "Remember, this is T-Bone we're talking about and strangers are just friends he hasn't met yet."

We all started to laugh until we heard T-Bone say, "Aunt Pat, Uncle Bob, what are you doing here?"

Chapter Four

Which One Is My Good Friend, T-Bone?

The next morning T-Bone and Wanda came over so we could call Eddie. I was worried he may have forgotten about us, but then I remembered that no one forgets T-Bone. It was part of his charm.

"Hi Mr. um, Mr. Fire, I mean Mr. Ed," T-Bone began, once again stumbling over his words. "I mean Edward or Edwin. Sorry, but you didn't really specify. Oh wait, is it Eduardo?"

"Just Eddie," he laughed. "So how are you kids doing?"

"We're good," said Wanda, quickly replacing T-Bone as our lead speaker. "We were hoping we could get the names of those firehouses and firefighters you suggested we visit."

"I actually just spoke to Wayne about that," he said. "So, even though you're already familiar with the Trenton Fire House, Wayne would like you to pay them another visit."

"Sounds great-tabulous," T-Bone said. "I mean awesome-ful."

"He means we'd be happy to," Wanda intervened. "What else have you got?"

"We thought Atlantic City would give you a good perspective of firefighting at the Jersey Shore," he continued. "Then we thought Vineland for South Jersey and my department, Union Township, for North Jersey. What do you think?"

"It sounds exciting," I said, hoping he would forget T-Bone was even on the call.

"Great," Eddie replied. "I know it's short notice, but Wayne is working today. If you can get to Trenton Fire Headquarters, I'll let him know you're coming."

"We'll take it," T-Bone yelled without even knowing if we had a ride. "Sold!"

"He means we'd love to," Wanda interrupted and motioned for T-Bone to stop talking. Unfortunately, he thought she meant keep talking.

"Since firefighters usually sit around the firehouse all day long, do we have to call first?" asked T-Bone.

"He didn't mean that," I said. "T-Bone's just joking."

This time I pushed him off the ottoman and onto the floor.

"Honestly kids, even with an appointment, there's a good chance they'll get called out at least once while you're there."

"As long as they leave someone there to keep an eye on the chili," said T-Bone.

"Keep an eye on what?" Eddie asked.

"More jokes," Wanda said as I pulled T-Bone into the kitchen. Wanda took care of the details and finished the call while I kept T-Bone out of range. When she entered the kitchen, she looked like her head was about to explode. I thought for sure she was going to start yelling at T-Bone, but instead she just stared at him. Not a normal stare and not even one of my mom's award-winning stares. No, this was much more than you're in trouble. And poor T-Bone had no idea what to do. The longer she stared, the more he fidgeted. Finally, she started to speak in what was, most likely, the quietest voice I had ever heard.

"T-Bone," she began, "in case you aren't aware of it, almost everything you have been saying to and about the firefighters has been rude and insulting. So, I'm going to say this one time and one time only. When we visit firehouses and speak to fire-fighters, the only thing I want to hear you say is, wow and thank you and nothing else. I don't want to hear about dalmatians, chili, or kittens in trees. I just want you to say *wow* and *thank you.* Are we clear?"

I had never been more afraid of another kid in my entire life. I wasn't even in trouble, yet we both stood there frozen. I couldn't remember a time that Wanda was this frustrated. As soon as she finished, she quietly walked back into the family room and sat on the couch. T-Bone and I just looked at each other.

"Maybe you should go home and come back later," I whispered. "Give her a minute to cool off."

"Are you crazy?" he said with a giant grin. "Did you just see that?"

"Yeah, I saw that," I answered. "She's really mad at you."

"She's not mad," he explained. "She's in love."

"In love?" I shrieked. "That's what you took from all of that? That she loves you?"

"Nicky, Nicky," he said, "don't you know hate isn't the opposite of love. Indifference is the opposite of love. Well, my friend, that wasn't indifference. That was passion. She loves me."

"Unfortunately," I said, "I think you're reading this completely wrong. I don't think she's in love with you, I think she's furious with you. There's a big difference."

"On the contrary," he replied, "they're almost the same thing. But, you go in there and I'll be right back."

"Where are you going?" I asked, hoping he wasn't about to make the situation worse.

"It's all under control," he said with a wink. "I'll be back."

While T-Bone left, I worked up the courage to return to my own living room. Wanda looked up, rolled her eyes, and shook her head. I rolled my eyes and shook my head in agreement. I called my grandfather to see if he was interested in visiting Trenton Fire Headquarters. Pop was a sucker for a shiny fire truck and quickly agreed. Before I could call T-Bone to tell him we had a ride, he was back in my kitchen. I ran back into the kitchen to join him.

"Nick, I was gonna run out and buy her flowers, but then I got a better idea," he whispered. "Watch this."

"Wanda," he said as he entered the living room, "I listened to everything you said and, even though your tone was a little disturbing, I agree with everything you said. Going forward, I won't say anything except *wow* and *thank you*."

"What's the catch?" she asked.

"No catch," said T-Bone, winking again."You have my honest assurance that I will be on my best behavior. Scout's honor. That means it's for real."

"Were you ever a scout?" she asked. "Because if you weren't a scout, that doesn't even count."

Pop walked in before things could get any weirder and asked if we had eaten lunch. This was another reason I loved summer. He suggested we stop at Pete's Steakhouse, one of our favorite places. This was an extremely easy question to answer. We also decided to stop by the State House, too, and let Billy in the Governor's Office know what we were working on. Maybe providing safety tips would finally get us elevated to Official Junior Ambassadors. If it took much longer, we'd be Senior Citizen Ambassadors by the time we were elevated.

We pulled up and could smell the steaks from the parking lot. Coming from Philly, I considered myself quite the cheesesteak connoisseur, and these cheesesteaks were great. When we walked in, we saw our old friends and the owners, Rich and Gina Tonti. I really loved all of the family businesses we visited. After a few minutes of catching up, our order was placed. There was nothing left to do except count the minutes until our food arrived.

As usual, T-Bone spoke loud enough to make sure everyone in our section knew that we were New Jersey's Unofficial Junior Ambassadors. A table filled with people who looked like they were on a lunch break made the mistake of responding to him.

"That's very nice," said one of the women. "We're all big fans of New Jersey. In fact, we work for NJM."

"NJM?" I asked.

"New Jersey Manufacturers Insurance Company," another woman said. "I'm Theresa and this is George and Paul."

"You guys manufacture insurance?" asked T-Bone. "Like in a factory? Very cool."

"No," Paul said as he laughed. "We insure things like cars and homes and we do our best to keep people safe."

"Oh," T-Bone replied, sounding disappointed that they didn't work at an insurance factory. "How can an insurance company keep people safe? Do you send your workers to their houses to remind them to turn off the stove and things like that?"

"Well," said George, "our customers might find that a bit intrusive and even creepy, you know, hanging around their houses and monitoring their actions."

"You have a good point," T-Bone agreed. "Having insurance people in your house would be weird, but you could totally put them in their cars. Then as they're driving, your people could say things like slow down, you're too close to that car, or how about using your blinker?"

"Wow," Theresa said, "those are very specific suggestions. How did you think of those so quick?"

"I didn't," T-Bone admitted. "That's just what my mom says to my dad every time we're in the car."

I had never been in the car with T-Bone's parents, so I couldn't confirm that those were the things his mom said to his dad,. I could, however, confirm that this was just a small sampling of what my mom said to my dad every time we were in the car.

"Very helpful," said T-Bone. "We're actually doing a report on safety and talking to firefighters across the state. Do you wanna help us?"

"We'd love to," said Theresa. "Here's my card. Call me and I can send you some very important safety tips."

"Thank you," said T-Bone as he stood there staring at them.

"This is getting really weird," Wanda whispered. "Why isn't he moving? Do something, Nick."

"I am doing something," I whispered back. "I'm enjoying it."

The standoff lasted over a minute and then Pat finally said, "Well, it was nice to meet you. I look forward to your call."

"Ditto," said T-Bone as he continued to stare.

"Is there anything else?" George asked.

"Restaurants are filled with potential accidents and injuries," said T-Bone. "I was just waiting for you to give me the all-clear. You know, that it's safe to return to my table."

"Oh," they all said, looking at each other somewhat relieved.

"Let's see," said Paul, "it looks like there are no speeding servers or trays filled with hot foods, so I'd say you're safe to return."

"Did you check for children who may be running," he asked.

"Sure did," said Paul, "I don't see any small children running."

"Thanks, then I will safely return to my table." said T-Bone. "And you should reconsider giving your customers insurance buddies to point out danger. I've never had such peace of mind in my life."

That peace of mind didn't last long. Sadly, he didn't notice his shoelace was untied. Poor T-Bone, after all of those safety checks, his first step turned into a giant face plant.

The happy smiles on the NJM faces morphed into shock as T-Bone hit the floor. Luckily, he immediately jumped up and yelled, "I'm alright, I'm alright."

Back at our table, there was less shock. Thanks to spending so much time with T-Bone, it would take a lot more than a *Three Stooges-style* fall to shock us. Plus, our food was being delivered and I could think of no better distraction.

We finished our meal, said good-bye to the NJM table, and headed to the State House. When we told Billy our idea, he agreed that it could be valuable for kids and adults. Then he had his own idea. "Hold on," he said. "You guys worked with New Jersey's Forest Firefighters when you were exploring the State Parks and Forests, right?"

"We sure did," said T-Bone. "They were awesome."

"The parks and forests, or the firefighters?" Billy joked.

"All of the above," I answered for T-Bone.

"Well, one of them is here right now," Billy continued. "Would you like to speak with him?"

"That would be fantastic," said Wanda. "They were so helpful last time, and it definitely wouldn't hurt to remind everyone about the dangers of forest fires."

Billy made a quick call and a moment later, Firefighter Quincy Jones came in. He had a big smile and immediately put everyone at ease. We took his information and he offered to meet us at a state park to go over some important safety tips. Wow, I thought to myself, this is really shaping up to be a thing.

When we arrived at Trenton Fire Headquarters, we didn't see any firefighters in hammocks as T-Bone predicted. Instead, there was one firefighter in a small office facing Perry Street called the watch desk. Unless there's a big emergency, someone is always manning that desk to respond to the community.

"Hi, we're here to talk to Wayne," I said. As soon as I said it, I realized the firefighter at the desk was Akyise Watkins. He was a huge help when we did our Code Read program in Trenton.

"Hey, you're from the book project," he said. "How are you?"

"We're good," said Wanda. "We're working on a safety report and we're here to meet with Wayne."

"Oh, you mean Captain Wolk?" he said.

"Yup, Captain Wayne Wolk," said T-Bone. "We're good friends. We go way back."

"Unfortunately, they may be a while. They were just dispatched to a careless cooking call," he explained.

"Careless cooking?" asked T-Bone. "That seems kind of minor. It sounds more like an issue for a cooking school than a fire department."

"Actually, a lot of housefires start out as minor careless cooking fires," said firefighter Marissa Bergen. "How people respond to it makes all the difference."

"So, if someone carelessly adds salt to their recipe instead of sugar, or burns their toast, they should call 9-1-1?" asked T-Bone. "Seems excessive, but if you say so."

"No," said Marissa. "Careless cooking fires are often fires that start when something people are cooking is left unattended or say, grease splatters near an open flame. It's not recipe mix-ups."

"Oh good, because last week I helped my dad make pancakes and grabbed the wrong canister," said T-Bone. "Instead of adding sugar, I added salt. Don't worry, though, we didn't call the fire department."

Suddenly, we heard the heavy sounds of approaching fire trucks. A moment later, Captain Wolk descended from the front passenger seat of Rescue One.

"Captain Wolk, you have some visitors, here," said Akyise. "Including your very good friend, T-Bone."

"That's great," said Wayne as he slowly peered over his glasses. "Now, which one is my very good friend, T-Bone?"

"I am," T-Bone said, raising his hand.

"There's my good friend," Wayne said with a wink. "Let me get the hammocks out and the cotton candy machine going. You're just in time for our carnival hour."

"Told you Hollywood pumps firefighting up for ratings," said T-Bone. "I mean, they have a cotton candy machine."

Wayne hung up his gear and a moment later he apologized for not being there. "Sorry, I'm late," he began. "We were out responding to a culinary mishap."

"That sounds dangerous," said T-Bone, "way more dangerous than a careless cooking call."

"That's just another name for careless cooking," said Wayne. "But the homeowner did the right thing by calling us first. When people try to put the fire out themselves, they often lose control of it."

He led us to the kitchen where we could sit down and take notes. The kitchen was really quiet, and I was sure T-Bone was still looking around for the cotton candy machine.

A Firefighter named Raul DelValle walked in, introduced himself, and offered us some snacks.

"No thanks," said T-Bone. "I'm waiting for the cotton candy."

"You're waiting for cotton candy?" he laughed. "Where? Here?"

"Wayne says we're in time for carnival hour," said T-Bone.

Raul looked confused.

"My good friend, Sirloin over here, thinks firefighting is hyped up for Hollywood," said Wayne.

"It's actually T-Bone, sir," he said. "My name is T-Bone, it isn't Sirloin."

"Hyped up, Pork Chop?" Raul asked T-Bone. "How so?"

"It's T-Bone," he repeated. "And, I think you're brave, but you probably spend most of your day hanging out or going to…"

"Let me guess," said Raul, "kitten in a tree calls?"

"Exactly," said T-Bone. "He gets it."

"So, let me ask you this," he responded, "have you ever seen a kitten spend his whole life in a tree?"

"No, why?" T-Bone replied.

"I'll answer it for you," said Raul. "You don't, because kittens eventually make their way down."

"Wow, so without saving kittens you do even less work than I thought you did?" said T-Bone, totally missing the point.

Before T-Bone could say another word, Wanda kicked him under the table.

"Owww," he exclaimed, until Wanda glared at him. "I mean wow and thank you."

The remainder of our visit was very informative, especially without T-Bone's constant interruptions and insults. Wayne used a rapid-fire question and answer method and I began.

"How long does it take to become a firefighter?" I asked.

"About 4-5 intense months in the fire academy," he answered.

"What calls does a city like Trenton get most?" asked Wanda.

"The highest number of calls are EMS, or Emergency Medical Services," he began. "The highest number of non-EMS calls are for alarm activations that are usually caused by malfunctions, normal cooking, or accidental."

"Are alarms ever real fires?" asked T-Bone. Wanda turned to look at him and he immediately said, "Wow, thank you, are alarms ever real fires?" Wanda sighed.

"Absolutely," he said. "We treat every alarm like a confirmed fire. We only confirm it's a false alarm after we've investigated."

"Makes sense to always be prepared," I agreed. "Can you tell us about some of the challenges of fighting fires in a city?"

"How much time do you have?" Wayne said with a laugh. "Two of the biggest ones are probably age and density."

"Old thick people?" asked T-Bone. Wanda glared at him again. "I mean, wow, thank you, old thick people?"

Wayne stared for a moment, shook his head, and continued. "No, I mean old buildings that are awfully close together. We have lots of homes that are over 100 years old, and many are row homes on narrow streets."

"Why does that matter?" asked T-Bone, now ignoring Wanda. "If cars are in the way, you can just nudge them along, right? I don't have a license, but I'm pretty sure the bigger vehicle wins."

"Nudge them along?" Wayne gasped. "No, we don't nudge them along. As a rule, we try to never hit anything with fire trucks that cost hundreds of thousands of dollars. The problem with narrow streets is that they limit the number of apparatus that can get near the scene. That means our equipment is much farther away and everything takes longer. Remember, seconds can be the difference between life and death."

"I never thought about that," I said. "But at least with your sirens you don't have to wait for traffic."

"Believe it or not, we get stuck in traffic a lot," he explained. "Sometimes it's people failing to yield to emergency vehicles, sometimes there's no room for them to move over, and then we also have to stop for the light rail train."

"That definitely sounds challenging," said Wanda.

"How tall is your ladder?" asked T-Bone. "You have some pretty tall high rises, so I'm guessing it must be really long."

"Not as long as you would think," said a firefighter who was heading our direction.

"Guys, this is Captain Domenick Stillitano," said Wayne. "He's the Captain of Engine 3."

"Nice to meet you," we all said at the same time.

"So, you guys have ladder questions?" asked Domenick.

"If they do, they should ask a ladder guy." Raul laughed as he rejoined our group. "In case you're wondering, our tallest truck ladder is 100 feet long and can reach 8 stories and our ground ladder can reach three stories."

"How tall is your tallest building?" asked Wanda.

"We have buildings that are over 20 stories," said Raul.

"So, if there's a high-rise fire, you need to make all the people in the building climb down the ladder?" asked T-Bone. "How does that even work? Do people jump 12 stories to get to the ladder? Because that seems like it could be risky."

"Wrong! You don't jump 12 stories to a ladder," said another firefighter who approached us with a big smile. We recognized him from Code Read. It was Captain Rob Buzzetta. "The rules for a fire in high-rise are a lot different than the rules for a typical house fire."

"That's true," said T-Bone. "My house doesn't have an elevator. High-rise people are lucky, they can catch the elevator to safety."

"Wrong again," said Rob.

"How can that be wrong?" asked T-Bone. "If I lived in a high rise and there was a fire alarm, I definitely wouldn't take the stairs; especially if I didn't have a chance to properly stretch. That could be dangerous."

"Bad choices are also dangerous," said Domenick. "If you live in a high-rise, you want to stay in your apartment unless the fire is on your floor. Those buildings are actually constructed with fire-resistant materials, so your best bet is to stay put."

"I feel like this will be a silly question, but why is the elevator a bad idea?" asked Wanda.

"That's a good question and there are several reasons," said Rob. "Say you live on the 8th floor and the fire is on the 4th floor. If you get on the elevator, the doors may open up on the fire floor."

"Also," said Marissa, "firefighters are able to take control of the elevator and use it to move personnel around the building. We can't do that if civilians are using it."

"Plus, there are a lot of people living on each floor of a high-rise," said Wayne. "If they're on a floor that needs to evacuate, we want them to use the stairs instead of waiting in an elevator line."

"Makes sense," said T-Bone. "Our hotel in Myrtle Beach had a long elevator line every day. It was so annoying."

"A long elevator line on vacation is annoying," said Marissa, "but a long line in a high-rise with a working fire could be fatal."

"Yikes," said T-Bone. "I mean, wow and thank you."

Unfortunately, our conversation was interrupted when a call came in for multiple trucks. The radio was shockingly loud, and I soon realized why firefighters didn't sleep through nighttime alarms. It seemed safe to assume that when they were at work, they never got a good night's sleep. Now, we were watching what happens before the trucks roll out of the firehouse. I was amazed at how organized and calm everything was. They really were professionals.

"Sorry, guys, but we have a house fire with smoke showing and possible victims trapped," Wayne said as he ran to the truck and stepped into his bunker pants and boots.

"Wow, they really do leave quick," said T-Bone with a nod.

"At least we got most of our questions answered," said Wanda. "This was really helpful, especially for all of those kids who live in highrises."

"We didn't get all of our questions answered," said T-Bone.

"What question did we forget?" asked Wanda, paging through her notes.

"The most important one," said T-Bone. "Are they cancelling carnival hour or just postponing it?"

Chapter Five

A Single Chocolate Chip

The next day, when I told my parents about our visit, they admitted that they never knew why civilians shouldn't take the elevator during a fire. Luckily, my increasingly sassy younger sister, Maggie, offered to clear up any confusion.

"You have to save it for the firefighters to take," she said with a smirk and her hands perched upon her hips. "What if you take it and it opens up on the fire floor? Then what?"

As she walked away, we all stared at each other. "We really need to do something about that," my dad said, clearly referring to Maggie's attitude. My mom nodded in agreement.

"So, what's your next stop?" asked my dad. "Does it involve golf or a driving range?"

"That would actually be a nice break," I said.

"How about we go hit a bucket of balls?" he offered. "And then you can tell me the rest of your plans."

We headed to the Mansfield Golf and Learning Center on Route 68 in Mansfield. We went inside and my dad spoke to the owner and former PGA Pro, Mike Lanzetta. Next to him was one of Pop's best friends, John Ficcara and his dog, Little Rennie. I wondered if there was anyone in the world that my grandfather didn't know. It suddenly occurred to me that Pop and T-Bone were very much alike.

While my dad was talking, I decided to start hitting some balls. Actually, hitting was too generous of a term. What I was doing was more like chopping and missing. Clearly, my baseball skills were not transferring over to golf.

"You should adjust your grip like this and try loosening your shoulders," said the gentleman in the next stall.

"Who? Me?" I asked.

He smiled and said, "Yes, you. Unless you're trying to make the ball go sideways."

A moment later, he was standing next to me and showing me the best way to grip a golf club. I took a couple of swings and it really worked.

"It's a lot harder than it looks," I said with a shrug.

"You just need some practice," he said before he hit a monster drive.

"Is that how you got so good?" I asked.

"That, young man, is the secret," he said, extending his hand. "I'm Ed Benson. I'm the Executive Director of Trenton's First Tee Program."

"I usually only drink water," I said, shaking his hand, "but my mother and grandmother like tea, so congrats on being in charge of it."

He started smiling again. "No son, I mean tee, like a golf tee. It's a program to introduce kids to the sport of golf."

I couldn't believe I said that. It was such a T-Bone thing to say. This was one of those moments where I wished I could rewind, delete, and start over.

"That sounds like a great idea," I agreed. "I guess the younger you start, the better you golf."

"Well, that's true," he said. "But, believe it or not, I didn't start golfing until I was 30 and working at Johnson & Johnson as a member of the sales management team. The thing with golf, is that it's one of those sports you're never too old to play."

"Johnson & Johnson?" I asked. "We learned all about Robert Wood Johnson II when we were in New Brunswick. During the Great Depression, he kept all of his workers employed and even gave them a 5% raise. And even though he owned a big company, he wrote a letter to President Franklin Delano Roosevelt calling for a law to increase wages and reduce hours for all American workers. He was a good guy."

"Wow," he said. "I don't meet many kids who know about the company's history. That was very impressive."

"Actually, my friends and I are Unofficial Junior Ambassadors of New Jersey," I explained. "So, we find, visit, and report on real places and people."

"Very interesting, young man," said Ed. "And you still have time to drop by the range?"

"As you can tell by my swing, I don't come here nearly enough," I laughed. "Are there any golf courses in Trenton?"

"There's actually the Trenton Country Club on the border of Trenton and Ewing," he said, "but the community we serve lacks access to golf. We're trying to provide an opportunity."

"It's pretty cool that you want to share a sport with kids," I said. "Baseball's actually my game. I used to pitch."

"I enjoy baseball, too," he said. "And while we want our kids to succeed at golf, our program teaches them so much more. Our participants learn things like inner strength, understanding and managing their emotions, and conflict resolution. There's so much more to the game than just a score."

"That's really cool," I said. Then I suggested writing a report about First Tee of Greater Trenton. He thought that was a great idea and gave me his card. He suggested I go on their website and call him if I had any other questions. Then he winked and reminded me to adjust my grip. *Again.*

By the time my dad came over, there weren't many balls left in the bucket. Luckily, he bought another one. Ed Benson had just left so my dad took that stall. He watched me take a couple of swings and told me he was impressed. He said he thought I'd be chopping at the ball and hitting it sideways. He should have been here fifteen minutes ago, I thought.

"So, where's your next adventure?" asked my dad. "Or have we covered the whole state yet?"

"What do you mean?" I asked.

My dad laughed for a moment. "You kids have been to every beach, almost every state park and forest, tons of museums and historical sites, recreation areas, restaurants, and theme parks. Is there anything left to explore?"

"That's the thing about New Jersey," I explained. "When we lived in Philly, I thought New Jersey was this dumb little state attached to Pennsylvania and that place we had to drive through to get to the Jersey Shore or New York."

"And now?" my dad asked with a raised eyebrow.

"I really feel kind of dumb," I admitted. "Before we became

ambassadors, I had no idea how many cool things were in New Jersey. What's even crazier, is that every time I think we'll run out of new things to find, a dozen more pop up."

"So, what's next?" he asked.

"Well, T-Bone spoke to Eddie from the NJFMBA," I began, "and he said he would arrange visits to firehouses in Union Township, Vineland, and Atlantic City."

"It should be interesting," said my dad. "Those fire departments are all in the same small state, but each one probably handles a number of calls unique to their area."

"I guess you're right," I agreed. "Vineland is pretty wide open and kind of landlocked, Atlantic City is on the ocean, and Union Township is a densely populated town."

"And Trenton's a densely populated city that houses the state capitol complex and sits alongside the Delaware River," he said. "Firefighting really is unique for every city and town."

"Let's not forget the forest firefighters," I added. "In fact, Quincy from the state forest fire service is supposed to call later today. They definitely have a unique situation."

"I guess no matter where the department is located, there's one thing that's the same," said my dad, "it's a dangerous career."

"That's true," I agreed. "The men and women who serve in the fire service are definitely some of the bravest people."

When the bucket was empty, I thought we were going home, but I was wrong. Instead, we stopped at the Bordentown Creamery for some ice cream. It wasn't often that I got to hang out alone with my dad. Usually my mom, my brother, my sisters, or T-Bone and Wanda were around. When we got back home, we agreed not to mention the ice cream stop since we didn't bring any back for anyone else. Too bad we forgot all about Maggie, our part-time amateur detective.

"Hey, I smell ice cream," she said as soon as we walked in the front door. "Where's our ice cream?"

"What are you talking about?" my dad replied, trying not to give away our secret.

"You had ice cream," she said.

"Why would you think we had ice cream?" I asked, already sounding guilty.

"Because you did," she said as she crossed her arms. "You had chocolate-chocolate-chip, Nicky."

"No, we didn't," said my dad as he tried to walk into the kitchen.

"And you," she said while blocking the doorway, "you had strawberry with chocolate sprinkles."

"Maggie, if we had ice cream, we would have brought some back for everyone," he explained.

"So, if I can prove you had ice cream without us, you'll bring us to get ice cream right now?" she demanded.

Wow, the stakes suddenly got higher, I thought. I was looking at both of them and couldn't tell if she was bluffing or not. I also couldn't tell if my dad was gonna fold or continue to deny that we had ice cream. She looked pretty confident with her foot tapping and her arms crossed. I would've folded.

"Maggie, we went and hit some golf balls," he said. "That's it."

"So, if I prove you had ice cream, are you going to bring us to get ice cream?" she repeated.

"Yes, yes, yes," he said, shaking his head. "But I have to warn you, without video evidence, your case will be hard to prove."

Clearly, they've both been watching too many detective shows. This was starting to get good and I was happy to just sit back and watch. Honestly, there were times Maggie really scared me. She was like a street-smart adult shoved into a kid's body.

"You forgot about eyewitnesses," she said as she turned and stared at me. "Nicky, did you and dad get ice cream today?"

I stared at her so hard, I could feel a tear running down my cheek. She didn't flinch. I really wanted to blink, but I couldn't. This was all too much.

"No," I said, trying to make my lie sound confident. "We didn't have any ice cream."

"Oh really?" she asked as she got closer and pointed to my shorts. "And I guess this chocolate ice cream stain with a giant chocolate chip stuck to it just fell out of the sky and landed on your leg?"

"Wait, what?" I asked, feeling my face redden. And there it was, right on my shorts, a single chocolate chip stuck to a blob of chocolate ice cream. It was time to come clean. We were out of moves and it was time to admit the truth. At least, that's what I thought our next move was.

"Nick, when did you get ice cream?" asked my dad, totally throwing me under the bus. "Not cool getting ice cream for just yourself, Nick. Do better next time."

I was shocked. All that father and son bonding and it just took one scary, irate little girl to undo it all.

"Don't bother, Nicky," she said, sounding like a TV prosecutor. "I've got this. I'll now present Exhibit B."

She walked right up to my dad and pointed to a prefect pink circle on his white golf shirt. It wasn't super noticeable, but once it was pointed out, it was impossible to deny. She stared at my dad without saying a word. There would be no closing argument, just the deafening silence and laser stare of a kid who proved her case beyond a reasonable doubt. A moment later my dad said, "Okay, Sherlock Holmes, go get everyone else."

And with that, a very proud Maggie headed to the car basking in her victory. When my mom asked why they were running out for ice cream in the middle of the afternoon, my dad just shook his head and said, "Long story."

Having already had ice cream, I decided to pass and stay home. That turned out to be a good decision, as Quincy called and invited us to meet him at Rancocas State Park the next morning. I called my friends and then asked Pop if he felt like going on another adventure. As usual, he agreed right away.

The next morning, we left bright and early. It wasn't a long drive, but Pop wanted to beat the heat and the traffic. My mom packed a cooler with cold drinks and sandwiches and sent along a bag with chips and snacks. I was hoping we wouldn't get lost, but if we did, we definitely had enough provisions.

Quincy greeted us with his usual smile and suggested we all take a deep breath.

"Smell that?" he asked.

"I don't smell anything," said T-Bone.

"Exactly," said Quincy. "That's how we like it; no smoke, no fire. We love nice, fresh air."

In the past, we included lots of forest fire information in our reports, but this was definitely worth repeating. Quincy agreed and brought us over to his truck.

"This is my fire truck," he said proudly. "It's definitely different than the fire trucks that protect your cities and towns."

"It sure is," said T-Bone. "You're missing the ladder and the bubble for the firefighter who steers the back."

"There's a good reason for that," said Quincy.

"Forest firefighters are better drivers and don't need a back helper?" asked T-Bone.

Quincy laughed. "They use those ladders to get to the top of buildings and in windows, right? Well, we don't really have tall buildings and windows in the forest. Now, look at the ground."

We all looked, although we weren't sure what to look for.

"What do you see?" he asked.

"A really cute fuzzy green caterpillar," said T-Bone, going in for a closer look. "He's adorable. I think I'll name him Green Bean. Hello, Mr. Green Bean."

"I see uneven terrain with rocks and tree stumps," said Wanda, ignoring T-Bone and Mr. Green Bean. "Also, there are no clear paths and lots of obstacles."

"Very observant," said Quincy as he tapped his foot on a tree stump. "And you're correct. The terrain is totally different. So, getting around in a forest requires a different type of vehicle."

"Like a golf cart with monster wheels," guessed T-Bone, "or an army tank? Or maybe some kind of transformer vehicle. Or even better, a hovercraft."

Quincy shook his head. "Moving along," he said, "generally speaking, how do firefighters put out most fires?"

"With water or fire extinguishers?" I asked.

"Yup, that's the plan," he agreed. "Do you guys remember what we use?"

"Well, you use water trucks and sometimes planes," answered Wanda, "but I remember learning that it's really hard to get water into a forest."

"Indeed," said Quincy. "That's why we use other tactics that wouldn't work in communities."

"Like infrared cameras that can detect people in the dark?" asked T-Bone.

"Well, they're really helpful for our brothers and sisters who serve in communities," he explained. "In a building, filled with black smoke, infrared cameras allow them to see someone who may be in trouble. Our situation is a little different."

"Last time, we learned how you use the dirt to stop a fire," I began. "It sounded crazy then, but now it makes sense."

"It's definitely a hard concept to grasp, especially for kids," said Quincy. "Most people expect water to be the only response."

"That's true," I said. "I used to think water was used for all fires. Then we learned that sometimes water can make a fire worse, like a grease fire. That's also why the different classes of fire extinguishers are labeled *A, B, C,* and *D.*"

"Correct," said Quincy. "An *A* extinguisher contains water, the *B* and *C* extinguishers contain powder for flammable liquids or electrical fires, and *D* are designed for use on flammable metals. Then you have the ones that are rated for multiple types of fires, like an *AB*, *BC*, or *ABC* extinguisher."

"Are they hard to use?" asked Wanda.

"Not at all," said Quincy. "Most use the PASS technique."

"Does that mean pass it to someone who knows what they're doing?" asked T-Bone.

Quincy laughed. "No, PASS means Pull, Aim, Squeeze, Sweep. You pull the pin, aim the extinguisher at the base of the fire, squeeze the handle, and sweep the nozzle from side to side."

"Do you go to the same fire academy?" I asked. "You know, as the firefighters who protect communities."

"Nope, there are too many differences," said Quincy. "If we went to their academy, we'd learn a lot of things we never use in wildlands while missing many of the skills we really need. And the same would be true if they went to our academy."

"So, it's like a doctor?" I suggested. "How some doctors go to regular medical school, and some go to specialized medical schools, like optometrists and dentists?"

"Exactly," said Quincy. "And then within the departments, you also have specialists like special rescue crews and hazardous materials teams."

I never thought about it that way. When you're a kid, all of the firefighters you see, from toys to books to costumes, are the traditional community firefighters. We never really learn about all the other kinds of firefighters or all the specialties. We realized one thing now, regardless of whether a firefighter was career, volunteer, community, or wildland firefighter, they all had one thing in common: they were all really brave and very special people.

Chapter Six

Just Like Magellan

When it came to community and forest firefighters, both worked to prevent fires, fight fires, and to save the lives and property of others. They just did it in such different ways.

Now, we were about to explore Rancocas State Park. Quincy gave us some good tips, although the only thing T-Bone was focused on was the cooler and the snack bag. Having a friend with such a rigid eating schedule wasn't always the most convenient way to explore. Luckily, Pop was more patient about T-Bone's eating habits than my dad would have been.

We drove down a long, winding gravel road and ended up at a small parking area. We decided to eat our lunch by the car, pulled out the park map, and highlighted the route we planned to take. Luckily, it was a cool, overcast day and wouldn't be too hot for my grandfather. In addition to the paper trail guide, Wanda pulled up the digital map and I opened the GPS step counter on my phone. I always liked seeing where I walked and how far.

We initially took the blue Creekside Trail which followed the Rancocas Creek pretty closely. There were other trails like Great Horned Owl and Oak Ridge that peeled off of Creekside. Pop suggested we take the Great Horned Owl trail, as it was a loop that brought us back to the blue path and the parking lot.

"This is so rustic," said Wanda. "I really love hiking in parks and forests that are untouched."

"I agree," said T-Bone. "This probably looks like it did when we were still a colony."

"You're right," said Pop. "With almost nine million people living in New Jersey, there's been so much growth and development. When you see places like this park or rolling farmlands, you should really appreciate them."

"Look," I said, pointing to the trail map. "The Rancocas Creek runs through the middle of the park. Check this out, the rest of the park is on the other side of the creek."

"You know," said Pop, "the other side also has its own trails and a nature center. And the two sides aren't connected."

"Hold on," I said. "There's also Long Bridge Park and the Hainesport Municipal Park."

"That's a lot of state parks," said T-Bone.

"Nope," said Wanda. "Long Bridge is a Burlington County Park and Hainesport is the local town park."

"I like how they're so close to each other," said T-Bone. "It's amazing how they ended up so close."

"Less amazing," said Pop, "and more strategic planning."

"Wow, we should probably head this way," said T-Bone as he stared up at the treetops.

"Why's that?" asked my grandfather.

"Quincy said there was a great view up ahead as the crow flies," explained T-Bone. "And a bunch of crows just flew by in that direction. We'll be just like the sailors who used to use stars to guide them."

"What?" I asked.

"Quincy told us to explore as the crow flies," said T-Bone.

"That's not even close to what he meant," said Wanda. "Did you really think he meant for us to follow random crows around a state park for a good view?"

"Listen, I don't make the rules," said T-Bone. "And, if Quincy said follow the crows, then I'm gonna follow some crows. I'll be like the Magellan of Mallards."

Wanda sighed and said, "Mallards are ducks."

Pop had heard enough. "So, a few things," he interjected. "Let's start with the fact that those birds weren't even crows, they were sparrows."

"My bad," said T-Bone, "is there an expression for following sparrows? Maybe that's what the great explorers used during the day when they couldn't see the stars."

"No, Tommy," said Pop, shaking his head, "explorers didn't use birds to chart their courses. How could they? They used stars because they're fixed in the sky. Birds don't stay in one place."

"That's why they're called the *Great Explorers,*" said T-Bone. "Any sailor could use the stars, but it took the impeccable skill of a Great Explorer, like Magellan, to navigate using birds."

"Fun fact," said Wanda, "the expression as the crow flies means the shortest distance without obstacles, as if you could fly somewhere."

"No, I'm pretty sure Quincy meant let the crows guide your journey," T-Bone insisted. "It's also very Zen."

"That sounds like the fortune you get at a boardwalk vending machine," I said laughing. "Or a message on a popsicle stick."

"They're called words of wisdom," T-Bone insisted. "Like: look before you leap or six dozen of one, half dozen of the other."

"It's six of one, half dozen of the other," Wanda once again corrected him.

"No, I'm pretty sure it's six dozen of one, half dozen of the other," said T-Bone.

"Nope, wrong, again," said Wanda. "The whole idea is when things are basically the same. A half dozen is six, so they're both the same."

"I'll have to look that up and get back to you," he conceded, but not before adding, "that would be like comparing apples and apples instead of apples and oranges."

Wanda took a deep breath and then she started counting.

"Speaking of apples," I interrupted, "look at these beauties my mom packed. Nothing like a firm red apple, am I right?"

I couldn't tell if Wanda and T-Bone were about to get into a real argument or if this was just banter. Pop wasn't going to wait to find out.

"I'll tell you what," said Pop in a subtly sarcastic voice, "we'll use the map today and maybe next time we come here, we'll let random birds lead us through a state park."

T-Bone looked up at the sky and said, "That's probably a good idea. I don't see too many crows in the vicinity."

"Or any crows," my grandfather whispered and shook his head.

As we headed back to the car, we weren't tired. We were actually energized. After a quick snack, Pop had an idea. Without telling anyone where we were going, he pulled up at Smithville Park in Burlington County. We came here a lot when we were *off-duty* because this was one of my parents' favorite parks.

"Historic Smithville Park?" asked T-Bone. "I love this place. My older brothers had to come here for their prom pictures. It's definitely a great setting for prom pictures, isn't it Wanda?"

Wanda didn't answer. She knew she had three years of T-Bone hinting about taking her to the junior prom to look forward to and it appeared her strategy would be to ignore him. T-Bone's strategy was to double down and ask more.

Like Long Bridge Park, Smithville was part of the Burlington County Parks System and like Rancocas State Park, there were two sides to this park. Except, unlike Rancocas, the split was due to a road and not a creek. There were other differences, too. Smithville Park had the rustic Smith's Woods section on the East side of Smithville Road. It was a scenic walk and part of it followed the Rancocas Creek. There were also restrooms, picnic tables, and a playground. On the west side were remnants of a former mill and industrial complex.

"Listen to this," said Wanda as she read the brochure. "The small mill grew into an industrial plant that employed hundreds of workers in its shops and yards from the 1860s to the 1920s. Known for its high-quality woodworking machinery, Smithville was ahead of its time when it came to things like town planning, sustainability, and workers' rights and welfare."

"Sounds like Robert Wood Johnson would've approved," I said.

"Definitely," said Wanda as she continued reading. "It also says that within its borders, it offered its residents and workers a variety of recreational, artistic, and educational opportunities. It was, in just about every way, the model industrial town."

As we explored the west side, we saw the Mansion Complex and the Farm Complex. It included the workers' homes and a Visitor Center. I tried to imagine growing up here. Then we saw Smithville Lake and the floating trail. Across this 22-acre lake was a 600-foot floating walkway and it was awesome.

A moment later, as we completed the floating trail and headed uphill, T-Bone started to dance. It looked strange, as there was no music. What was stranger was his choice in dance moves. It was a combination of robot and dancing inflatable. We all stopped walking and stared.

"What's he doing?" Wanda whispered.

"Trying to impress you?" I guessed.

Before we could ask him, he was rolling around on the ground. I looked at Pop and he just shrugged. He had spent so much time with T-Bone that he knew better than to get alarmed at the first weird dance. After a minute, he stopped rolling, grabbed his water and began pouring it all over his head.

"He's clearly not on fire," Wanda whispered, "yet he stopped, dropped, and rolled and now he's pouring water on himself."

"I was thinking the same thing," I agreed. "I'm so confused."

"Nick, Nick, hand me your water," T-Bone yelled as he rolled around. "I need your water. I need every drop of it."

"I don't think so," I said.

"Wanda, Wanda, toss me your water," he pleaded.

"No way," she said. "And if this is some sort of interpretive dance prom-posal…"

"Interpretive dance?" he shrieked. "This isn't a prom-posal, it's an emergency."

"What's the emergency?" I asked, still not convinced.

"I walked into a spider web, Nick!" he yelled. "My face walked into a web. I'm covered in web."

Wanda and I couldn't help but start laughing. When I finally caught my breath, I extended my hand to pull him up. "This is just because you walked into a spider's web?"

"*Just walked into a spider web*?" he gasped. "Did you see the size of that web? It was size of a small car. That thing was huge."

As soon as Pop realized what was happening, he pulled out a handkerchief and a bottle of water. When he grabbed T-Bone's baseball cap, T-Bone noticed the spider.

"That's him," he yelled. "That's the spider."

We thought he was afraid, but instead he leaned down and said, "I'm sorry I wrecked your house. It was an accident."

"Are you apologizing to a spider?" I asked.

"Nick, I destroyed his home," said T-Bone. "And it was an enormous home. I feel terrible. He looks so sad. He reminds me of Mr. Green Been."

"What do you want to do?" I asked. "Make him a new web?"

"Don't be ridiculous," said T-Bone. "I can't spin a web. Maybe we should look for another web and let him move there."

"I'm sorry, but what?" asked Wanda. "You want us to find an available web for the spider that made the web you walked into?"

"That's exactly what we should do," said T-Bone.

"I'm confused," said Pop. "You were rolling around like you were on fire because you're afraid of spiders and now you want to find him a new web."

"I'm not afraid of Sammy," said T-Bone.

"Who's Sammy?" I asked.

"The spider," T-Bone replied. "I named him Sammy."

"Okay," said Pop. "What was all the dancing and rolling around about if you aren't afraid of spiders?"

"Oh, that?" he asked. "I'm not afraid of spiders, I'm terrified of *spider webs.* They really creep me out."

"Well, I don't think we're gonna find a vacant web for Sammy," said Wanda. "Plus, I'm sure he can have a new web whipped up in no time. Spiders are pretty quick."

"But I feel like I owe him something," said T-Bone. "You know, he is my newest friend."

"Your newest friend?" I asked.

"Sure," said T-Bone. "Animals can be friends."

"Oh, I agree that animals can be great friends," I said. "But I don't think you have to find your new friend a new web."

"Why's that?" he asked.

"Because he's starting a new web on your hat," I replied.

As soon as T-Bone realized what Sammy was doing, he placed his hat on the ground and slowly backed away. "Enjoy your new home, little Sammy. It's all yours now."

When he returned to the car without his hat, Pop immediately noticed. When T-Bone explained that he had given it to Sammy to make up for destroying his webby home, Pop stepped out of the car. He walked up to the hat, used a stick to slide Sammy to the ground, and blew the beginning of a web off the brim.

"Oh, no," T-Bone shrieked when Pop handed him the hat. "You took little Sammy Spider's home. Now what will he do?"

"He said to tell you thanks, but no thanks," said Pop. "Plus, I helped him out. The other spiders would have teased him if he lived on a hat. Now, he can be a real spider and make real webs."

"He spoke to you?" asked T-Bone. "With words or with his eyes? You know there are so many ways to communicate."

"Definitely with his eyes," said my grandfather as he tried to hold back his laughter. Then, he looked at me and Wanda, shrugged and rolled his eyes. Message received, I thought.

Chapter Seven

Bet Red, Kid, Bet Red

There was nothing more beautiful than New Jersey's State Parks and Forests. They were, however, also exhausting. We decided to spend a few days just relaxing after our trip to the parks. No reports, no visits, and no summer assignments, just lots of fun. Of course, that changed when Eddie and Wayne made plans for us to visit the Atlantic City Fire Department.

When T-Bone asked Wayne for some Atlantic City advice, Wayne said, "I'll tell you what I always tell my wife, Amy and my son, Chase. Bet red, kid, bet red."

"Wow, do you have secret insider knowledge?" asked T-Bone.

"Secret insider knowledge? Not at all," Wayne laughed. "But fire trucks are red, so always bet on red."

What I heard was, you can always count on the fire department, so always bet on them. No matter how dangerous the situation, you can bet they will be able to help you. Unfortunately, T-Bone decided to go with a more literal interpretation.

"So, do I just go up to the poker table and say put it all on red?" he asked.

"You're way too young to gamble," said Wayne. "Plus, your plan would never work. Betting on red and black is for roulette, not poker."

"Stick to the boardwalk," said Eddie. "You can never go wrong with some Jersey Shore pizza and soft ice cream."

"Good point," T-Bone agreed.

The very next day, we were heading down Route 206 toward Atlantic City. We arrived a little early, so Pop suggested we take a stroll on the boardwalk. It was warmer than our forest walk, but with a sea breeze, it didn't feel too bad. We headed toward the Steel Pier, filled with rides and amusements. It was hard to ignore all the history in Atlantic City. On our previous trips, we learned so much about the place most New Jerseyans refer to as AC. Even the boardwalk was historic as it was the very first boardwalk in America. Most people think they were created to provide people with places to walk, play games, and grab food. The real purpose was a little less exciting. In 1870, Alexander Boardman, a railroad conductor, needed a good idea to keep sand out of hotels and train cars. What most people didn't know is that the original boardwalk was removable and taken apart at the end of each season. I couldn't imagine being the guy who had to take a mile long boardwalk apart and then assemble it each year.

We walked until we came to the *In the Line of Duty Memorial.* The pillars representing the Twin Towers of the World Trade Center, the police officer, the police dog, and the kneeling firefighter were necessary reminders of the sacrifices made by first responders. It was important to honor those killed in the Line of Duty as well as the 9/11 First Responders. When most people go to work, the most serious threat they face is their commute. For First Responders, commuting was the least dangerous part of their shift.

Pop told us the 9/11 terror attacks were devastating. He said it was like the assassination of President John F. Kennedy or the explosion of the Space Shuttle Challenger – people always remember where they were and what they were doing. As the World Trade Center in New York City, the Pentagon in Washington DC, and Shanksville, PA were simultaneously attacked, no one really knew what was happening. The First Responders who answered the calls at all three locations, rushed in without knowing if there were more attacks coming. The shock of the attacks was compounded when the unthinkable occurred and the World Trade Center's 110-story Twin Towers collapsed. Altogether, 2,977 victims were killed, and thousands were injured. Flights were grounded and the country came to a standstill. The days after the attack were a flurry of emotion, fear, and anger. It was the deadliest terror attack in human history and the single deadliest incident for First Responders. The numbers were heartbreaking with 343 firefighters and 72 police officers killed. Those numbers, however, didn't include the illnesses and deaths experienced by the people who worked on the pile, looking for survivors and removing debris for months. Over 100 firefighters died from 9/11 related injuries and illnesses after the attack. And 2,100 had to retire on disability due to illnesses stemming from the wildly toxic dust at Ground Zero. He told us that day changed our country forever. Pop's explanation and the memorial made us appreciate First Responders even more.

As we continued our walk, a group of seagulls came in low and just missed T-Bone's head. "Your compasses are here," I joked. "Ask them which way to go, Ponce DeLeon."

"First, it's Magellan, not Ponce DeLeon," T-Bone replied. "And second, these birds aren't crows. They're thieves."

"Thieves?" asked my grandfather.

"Yup, thieves," T-Bone repeated. "The first time I came to the shore with Nick and his family, I opened the cooler and forgot to shut it. Those flying thieves stole our sandwiches. And you should've seen Mr. A's face. You know, sometimes he's wound a little tight."

"That was some Garden State Adventure we had," I laughed. "I thought my dad was gonna completely lose it that day."

"He didn't lose it that day?" asked a shocked T-Bone. "Are you sure? He looked pretty steamed."

"Not even close," I laughed. "You weren't around when we were packing up our house in Philly and moving to New Jersey. That day almost sent him over the edge. We waited forever for the moving company to arrive and when the truck for Ed's Reliable Movers pulled up, there was only one 75-year-old man driving it. The best part was when my dad asked if he was alone and Ed asked if our stuff was heavy."

"Hold on," said T-Bone. "Where were the movers? You know, the people who lift your heavy furniture?"

"That's what got my dad so steamed," I explained. "Ed said his older brother was having heart bypass surgery and his younger brother was fishing."

"Why would your parents hire that company?" asked Wanda.

"Coupons," said Pop. "I vaguely remember it involved a discount or a coupon."

"What did you guys do?" asked T-Bone.

"Some of my friends' fathers came to help. In fact, Bobby Boots' dad and uncle are firefighters. They happened to be off duty, so they helped us load and unload."

"Always bet on red," said T-Bone, "always bet on red."

"Look," said Pop as he walked up to the boardwalk railing that overlooked the beach. "Do you realize how lucky you are?"

"What do you mean?" I asked. "I mean, I know I'm pretty lucky, but what are you talking about?"

"This," my grandfather said pointing over the railing, "this magnificent ocean. You're so lucky to live in a coastal state. There are so many people who have never seen an ocean or heard the sounds of the waves crashing on the beach. They've never walked on warm sand or rode a breaking wave into the beach."

"Or smelled the warm salt air," added Wanda. "Or watched the seagulls walking on the beach."

"Thieves," said T-Bone.

"I agree," I said. "About the ocean, not the thieves. For a small state, we're lucky to have 127 miles of beaches."

"Remember, when we explored the whole Jersey Shore?" asked T-Bone as he turned to Wanda. "That was before you joined our group."

"Remember?" I asked. "How could I forget? We explored every beach town from Cape May to Keansburg. Actually, we ate our way from Cape May to Keansburg."

"Speaking of eating, let's grab some slices before we head over to the firehouse," Pop suggested.

We headed over to 3 Brothers From Italy for some pizza. Not only was Jersey Shore pizza delicious, but the slices were also enormous. We finished just in time to leave the boardwalk, but Pop needed to make one more stop. We headed to Fralinger's where Pop quickly bought a box of Saltwater Taffy.

"Sweet tooth?" asked T-Bone.

"More like sweetheart," Pop said with a wink. "They're my wife's favorite and taffy is definitely the way to her heart."

"Classy gesture," T-Bone replied as he looked at Wanda.

"Don't even think about it," she said.

The ride to the firehouse was very familiar. We had visited Atlantic City several times, but never really noticed all of the firehouses. Like in most towns, they kind of blended into the scenery. That is, until they came roaring out with their lights and sirens on.

We pulled up to the firehouse and were greeted by three firefighters. "Welcome to the Atlantic City Fire Department."

"Thanks for having us," I said. "We're excited to be here."

"I'm John Varallo Jr. from Rescue Company 1, this is Robert Scattone from Ladder Company 2, and this is Sylvester Fonville the Captain at Engine Company 5," said John. "Come on inside and we'll tell you a little bit about what we do and show you around."

"I have some questions," said T-Bone.

"Wow, you don't waste any time, do you?" said John. "Go ahead, what are your questions?"

"Well, first I wanted to know what type of video games you guys are currently playing," asked T-Bone. "Next, I want to know where you keep the dalmatians. And third, has your chili won any awards?"

"Did you guys bring chili?" asked Robert. "Because we've been out on runs all morning and we're starving."

"No," said a rather confused T-Bone, "I was talking about your daily pot of chili."

"Our daily pot of what?" asked an equally confused Sylvester.

"You know," T-Bone explained. "You're firefighters, right? That means you have dalmatians, you make chili every day for lunch or random cook-offs, you play video games, you take naps, you drive Santa around town, you bagpipe, and then you put out the occasional fire. So, has your chili won any major awards?"

The three Atlantic City firefighters were speechless. They stared at T-Bone and then looked at the rest of us. John started to say something, stopped and scratched his head. Finally, Sylvester looked at T-Bone and said, "Do you watch a lot of television?"

"I do," said T-Bone. "Just like firefighters. How did you know?"

"Lucky guess," he said. "Call it a hunch."

"So, you're pretty confident that you know about firefighting, are you?" asked Robert.

"Well, I don't like to brag," said T-Bone. "But I'd say I have a pretty solid grasp of the fire service. Except for the runs, I didn't realize you guys jog so much. Impressive."

"Interesting," said John. "How about we give you a tour and then you can look at our call log. And by the way, runs are when we leave the station to respond to a call."

"Oh, I knew that," said T-Bone with a slightly red face. "I was just testing you."

We took a tour around the station, saw the apparatus floor, and met the firefighters. When we arrived, most weren't playing video games or fetch with a dalmatian. They were in a class. Sylvester let us listen in and they were discussing hazardous materials and chemicals. It sounded complicated, but they all seemed to understand.

Our next stop was the kitchen and, ironically, there wasn't a big pot of award-winning chili ready for lunch or the random cook-off. The one thing I did notice was how clean it was. Everything was stainless steel and practically sparkled. My mom would've loved to cook in such a big kitchen.

"Are you still looking for the chili?" asked Robert. "Do you think we're holding out on you?"

"I was definitely looking for it, but the smell would've given it away," T-Bone replied. "So, you really don't always have five alarm chili ready to go?"

Sylvester shook his head. "There are days when we have so many calls, or runs that last for hours, that we don't even eat until late at night."

"But what if you have a very rigid eating schedule?" asked T-Bone. "Everyone knows I have to eat at 12:00 and 5:00."

"Really?" asked John. "What happens if you don't eat at that time?"

"I don't know," T-Bone admitted. "I never tried it. But I'm sure it wouldn't be good."

"I'll tell you what," Robert began, "I can guarantee you that if you're a firefighter with a rigid eating schedule and a run comes in during your mealtime, you wouldn't even remember you're supposed to be eating."

"It's true," said John. "We are so focused on responding that we forget about being hungry or tired. We just get right to work, day or night, hungry or not hungry."

"That's why Trenton's lucky to have Signal 22," he said.

"He means the Signal 22 Canteen Truck," I explained. "When they have a big call, the canteen truck arrives with the Signal 22 volunteers who provide things like coffee and donuts or even pork roll sandwiches."

When we finally finished talking about food, we moved onto what they do all day. As we were talking, I noticed so many things. Some guys were cleaning the trucks, others were putting things in the truck compartments, and some were cleaning the house. What I didn't notice was anyone goofing off or watching TV. And, there were definitely no hammocks or cotton candy machines.

"It seems like everyone's pretty busy," I said. "Like really busy. Does all this work make you tired when a call comes in?"

"Actually, when a call comes in, our adrenaline pumps and we don't feel tired," said Robert.

"But, boy when we get home from our shifts," Sylvester added, "we're exhausted."

"Is it hard to sleep at home since you're so used to waking up in the middle of the night at work?" asked Wanda.

"Very hard," said Robert. "You basically sleep with one eye open for your entire career."

"Your entire career?" said Wanda. "That's really not healthy."

"Not much about firefighting is healthy," said John. "Besides the obvious danger and the lack of sleep, there's also the toxins that we're exposed to regularly."

T-Bone was shocked. Toxins didn't sound very glamorous or very Hollywood.

"So here are the calls we've had for the past 24 hours," said Sylvester, pulling up a report on the computer. It was shocking. There were calls for alarms, careless cooking, the casinos, motor vehicle accidents – one with people trapped in the car, and even people stuck in a hotel elevator.

"Does this happen every day?" I asked. "Or would you call this a particularly crazy day?"

"We call that a slow morning," Robert laughed. "The rest of the calls are on the next screen."

"How do you fit in all of the fun stuff?" asked T-Bone.

"You do realize this is a job, right?" asked John.

"Oh, I get that," said T-Bone. "But your job is in a house, so you should be able to kick back."

"Do you have any advice for kids and parents that read our reports?" asked Wanda, trying to change the subject. "Things that will keep them safe which can then keep you safe."

"We have a lot of advice," Sylvester said with a smile. "Our city is only 10 square miles, but we have many unique challenges. For starters, there's the Atlantic Ocean. Then, there's the lengthy boardwalk, nine massive casinos, numerous hotels, old houses, row homes, high crime and poverty, and the 26 million annual visitors. Our advice is to always call 9-1-1 first, before things get out of hand."

"With how busy your shifts are, I would think you'd want less calls," I said.

"Well," Robert explained, "Even if a person isn't sure, we'd much rather have them call us to check out the situation. All too often people are afraid to call or think they can handle a situation themselves. The best course of action is to call us first. If it turns out to be nothing, we verify and return to quarters. But if it's something serious, when we arrive matters. Seconds can be the difference between living and dying."

"It's true," said John. "When people wait, by the time we arrive, things may be out of control."

"That's a good point," I said. "Are the casinos and high-rises also a big challenge? The firefighters in Trenton told us that their longest ladders are 100 feet."

"Absolutely," said Sylvester. "High-rise hotels are dangerous because the guests don't live there. Most don't realize that there are different rules for high-rises than for low rises. We want people to stay in their room or apartment unless the fire is on their floor. And, even then, we'll give them instructions. The worst scenario is to have people running all over the building."

"That sounds like it would be awful," said Wanda. "But to be honest, if I was staying in a high-rise and the alarm went off, I might panic and try to run out, too."

"It's human nature to run away from danger," said Robert. "That's why what you're doing will really help."

They continued to share more great tips, including those for water safety. Between the ocean and so many hotel pools, there are lots of opportunities for people to get injured, or even die. They recommended the buddy system for both. They said no one should ever swim alone and should always have a buddy. For the ocean they stressed never swimming when a lifeguard isn't present. The ocean has a strong undertow, or rip current, that pulls people out to sea, even strong swimmers. Staying in marked, guarded areas is extremely important to make sure a fun day at the beach doesn't end tragically.

"One thing the lifeguards constantly try to remind people is that if they find themselves caught in an undertow and being pulled out to stay calm," said Sylvester. "When people panic, they go under and often drown."

"What should you do?" I asked.

"Great question," said John. "The best thing to do is to swim along the coast as opposed to trying to swim directly to shore,"

"Really?" T-Bone asked. "Wouldn't it be quicker to just swim straight to shore? You know, a straight line like the crow flies."

"So, a rip current can quickly pull someone hundreds of yards from shore," said Robert. "The best way to survive is to stay afloat and yell for help, or swim parallel to the shore."

"This might sound awful, but what happens if someone finds themselves in trouble and goes under?" asked Wanda. "Who comes to help the lifeguards?"

"That's not an awful question, but it can be an awful situation," said Sylvester. "It's very serious when someone goes under and often results in a joint response between the ACFD, the New Jersey State Police, and the Coast Guard."

It was exhausting just listening to all the situations they needed to be prepared for. It was no wonder they trained and had drill school every day. The Atlantic City Fire Department definitely has its share of unique challenges, and no one was more surprised than T-Bone. We thanked everyone for their time and headed out to the car. Once inside the car T-Bone said, "I can't stop thinking about chili right now."

"Seriously?" asked Wanda. "For the millionth time, they don't have time to make pots of chili every day for lunch and random cook-offs."

"Obviously," said T-Bone, surprising all of us. "I don't know about other fire departments, but Atlantic City and Trenton definitely don't have time to make chili."

"Then why are you thinking about chili?" I asked.

T-Bone shook his head and sighed. "I was just thinking that we should send some chili to the firehouse *for them*."

Chapter Eight

Ike Seems Popular

When we returned from Atlantic City, I was wiped out. There was definitely something about the ocean air that made me sleep like a baby. It also made me wake up with a lot of energy. I decided to get a jump on the Atlantic City report while it was all fresh in my mind. As soon as I opened my laptop, Wanda walked in waving the report. I wondered if she ever really slept. I pictured her like some sort of robot that just charges herself for an hour every night. It was the only thing that could explain her crazy productivity.

T-Bone came in right behind her, followed by my grandfather. "Did I forget something?" I asked as the parade strolled through the living room.

"That depends," said T-Bone. "Did you brush your teeth?"

"No, I mean, did we plan a trip for today?" I asked. "Why are you all here? At once? In a line?"

"I just came by to bring my report," said Wanda.

"I just came by to see if anyone was free," said Pop.

"I just came by because I'm awake," said T-Bone. "And hungry. And this is what I do every day. It's kind of weird that you don't know this."

"Wait," I said, "Pop, you're inviting us on a trip?"

"Well, I wouldn't exactly call it a trip," Pop replied.

"Is it an adventure?" asked T-Bone. "Does it involve a water park? Or history? Or go-karts? Penguins? Possibly pirates?"

"No, it's not an adventure or any of those other things," said Pop. "I was thinking about going to go to Marsilio's Kitchen and thought I'd see if you kids wanted to join an old man for an early dinner."

"Who's the old man?" I asked with a shrug. "Because I don't see any old men here."

"Your grandfather is the old man," said T-Bone.

We all stared at him. "Seriously, T-Bone?" asked Wanda.

"What? Did I say something wrong?" he asked.

"Sure, we'd like to go," Wanda and I agreed.

"Where's Marsilio's Kitchen?" asked Wanda.

"It's Alan's restaurant in Ewing," Pop replied.

"Hmmm," she said, looking up and thinking.

"Was there a place in Ewing that you needed to visit?" asked Pop.

"If it's not a bother, and since it'll be so close, I was wondering if we could stop by The College of New Jersey."

"Sure," said Pop. "Thinking of applying early?"

"Wanda, is that where we're all applying to go to college?" asked T-Bone.

"*We're*?" Wanda replied.

"Sure," said T-Bone. "I always assumed the three of us would go to the same college, right? Why break up the band?"

"First of all," Wanda began, "we're just starting high school in the fall. That was a joke. And second, I don't think any of us know where we're going to college. It's a little early and we don't even know what we want to be when we grow up."

"Oh, I already know what we'll be," said T-Bone.

"This ought to be good," I said. "Go on. What we will be?"

"Well, Nick, I think you're going to be a judge," he began. "Nothing fancy like Supreme Court or Superior Court. Maybe like a traffic judge. Since you're a decent referee for Timmy and your sisters, you'll be a decent judge. Wanda, you're super organized and smart, so you'll be the Governor. Not the first female Governor of New Jersey, that was Christine Todd Whitman, but you'll definitely be the Governor."

"I'm considering a career in medicine," said Wanda.

"You could do both," said T-Bone. "Governor doesn't look that hard. You could probably be a full-time doctor and a part-time Governor and still have lots of time left over."

"So, that's not possible," I said. "You do realize the Governor has a really hard job, right? There's no way someone could be a governor and a doctor at the same time."

"Well, she'd definitely have to give up her Unofficial Junior Ambassadorship," said T-Bone.

Pop laughed. "If Wanda is elected governor, she'll actually be the number one Official Ambassador of New Jersey."

"Wait, I just have to get elected Governor to finally become official?" asked T-Bone.

"Yup, but then that'll mess up your plans for all of us," I laughed and then added, "Case dismissed."

"So, what makes you want to stop by TCNJ?" asked Pop.

"That's where my mom went to college and we go there a lot," Wanda explained. "Her birthday's coming up, so I wanted to get her a sweatshirt or a mug."

"Your mom went to The College of New Jersey?" I asked.

"Actually, she went to Trenton State College," said Wanda. "They changed the name after she graduated."

"How about we take a walk around the campus and then check out the store?" Pop suggested. "And since we're heading that way, I have one other stop that you might enjoy."

"Is it a water park?" asked T-Bone. "Or a zoo? Please say it's a glow-in-the-dark bowling alley."

"I'll leave this one as a surprise," said Pop.

My grandfather had some tea with my mom and then we were on our way. T-Bone was so excited to have a mystery stop, he couldn't stop guessing where we were going.

"The Adventure Aquarium?"

"Nope," said Pop.

"Six Flags?"

"Nope."

"Golf and/or mini golf?"

"Nope and nope."

"Deep sea diving?"

"Wow, nope."

"Will you tell me if I get it right?" asked T-Bone.

Instead, Pop stopped the car and said, "We're here."

"Where are we?" I asked. "And why did you stop the car in the middle of the street?"

"We're at Italian People's Bakery. It's a Trenton institution," said Pop with a big smile. "And this is called double parking."

"Double parking?" I asked. "Is this legal? It doesn't feel legal."

"It's kind of grandfathered in," said Pop. "It's a Chambersburg tradition."

"So only grandfathers can do this?" I asked, still shocked that we were leaving the car in the actual lane. "And how long can we keep the car in the lane?"

"Nope, not just for grandfathers," said Pop. "People pull up to stores or in front of their home to unload things like groceries and then they find a parking spot. And, no need to worry, we'll only be a few minutes."

We could smell the bakery as soon as we stepped out of the car. It was an awesome combination of fresh bread and cake. We followed Pop through the left front door like a row of baby ducklings. Once inside, we turned into tourists as we pointed at each section of the glass case.

"Hey, Matt, how are you?" Pop said to the man standing behind the counter.

"Good to see you," said Matt. "Who did you bring with you?"

While Pop introduced us, Matt Guagliardo came out and shook our hands and asked what we were in the mood for. I wanted to say everything because I couldn't decide. T-Bone just stared at the donuts. Wanda, however, knew exactly what she wanted.

"Strawberry cheesecake, please," she said without hesitation.

"You've got it," said Matt. He then turned to me, "And how about you?"

"The walnut brownie," I said, my mouth already watering.

"I guess that leaves you," Matt said to a very confused T-Bone. "Did you decide yet?"

"Yes," said T-Bone. "I'll take the glazed donut because that's my favorite. No wait, I'll take the giant cupcake. Scratch that, I'll take the apple turnover. No, wait, the giant chocolate chip cookie. Oh, I don't know, I can never decide. How about I turn around and you surprise me."

"I'll tell you what," said Matt, "I'll give you an assortment and you can all try a little of each."

"That's a great idea," T-Bone said as he turned around. "Did you bake all of these things?"

Matt laughed. "No, that would be a lot of baking. We actually have a very talented staff, and it takes a lot of them to keep up with the demand."

"More than five?" asked T-Bone.

"We employ between 75-100 people," said Matt. "From our bakers, retail clerks, deli clerks, office staff and drivers."

"You can deliver?" asked T-Bone. "Like to my house? Because I'll give you my address right now."

"Well, we deliver to restaurants and stores," said Matt.

"We just visited a couple of restaurants that have really good bread," T-Bone began. "Have you ever heard of Rossi's Bar & Grill and Pete's Steakhouse? Their bread is amazing."

"I agree," Matt said with a smile. "We supply their bread."

"I knew it," I said. "My mom says it's the bread that makes the sandwich and Rossi's and Pete's have really good bread."

"It must be a lot of work to make so many baked goods and breads," said Wanda. "Did you start the bakery?"

"No," said Matt. "My great grandfather, Pasquale Gervasio, left Italy at 14 years old with his brother and stowed away on a boat headed to America."

"Wow," said T-Bone, "my mother didn't want me to cross the street by myself until I was 12."

"Yeah, it's hard to imagine," Matt continued. "And because they were stowing away, they had to survive on lemons for a two-week journey. Imagine that. Luckily, he made it and by 1936, with the help of his wife, Margaret and their five kids, he opened a bakery on Hamilton Avenue."

"Hold on," said T-Bone. "Isn't this Butler Street?"

"Yup, this is Butler Street, but it's not the original location," said Matt. "The business has changed and grown a lot over the years. In 1969, there was a bad fire. The oven was too close to the ceiling, and it wasn't vented properly. My dad was sleeping in the apartment upstairs. No one else was home and only one worker knew he was up there. That worker saved his life."

"Wow," I said, "your dad was so lucky. How long was the bakery closed to rebuild? Months? Years?"

Matt shook his head. "They found a vacant bakery, cleaned it up, and were baking bread the very next day."

"That's incredible," I said. "Now, how are you related to Pasquale and Margaret?"

"My grandmother, Phyllis, was one of their five kids. My dad, Carmen was her kid."

"So, you're the fourth generation," I asked, hoping I had counted right. "Like Joanna at Rossi's. When did you start working here?"

"I started working on Sundays, all day, when I was 12-years old," he said. "Back then, we had about 8 locations. My dad oversaw all of them and my mom worked in Mercerville."

"I have two questions," asked Wanda. "Are you and your dad bakers? And what's your favorite thing to eat here?"

"Absolutely," he said. "We both bake, but now, I'm the manager. And my favorite thing is bread. I could eat bread all day long."

"Is there a fifth generation that will take over?" I asked.

"Well, there's definitely a fifth generation," he said with a smile. "My wife, Heather, and I have two sons, Christian and Mason. But since they're only 8 and 11-years old, it's too soon to tell."

"I wish my family owned a bakery," said T-Bone. "Your kids are lucky. What's their favorite thing to eat?"

"It's funny," said Matt, "Christian takes after me and loves bread, while Mason loves cupcakes and glazed donuts."

"I'm totally team Mason," said T-Bone.

Matt then explained that his bakery is a 24/7 business. They bake bread and baked goods nonstop, and deliveries start rolling out at 11:00 pm for the next day. He told us that when his grandfather started the business, he'd make a certain number of loaves of bread every day. When he sold the last one, he closed. Whether that last one sold at noon or after dinner, he stayed open until it was gone.

"I would have paid my friends to buy the loaves early so I could have the rest of the day off," said T-Bone.

"That's not exactly a solid business plan," said Matt.

It took a moment and then T-Bone saw the flaw in paying his friends to buy his bread with his own money. Meanwhile, a woman named Carissa picked out some nice loaves of bread and rolls for my grandfather.

"Nice and warm," she said with a smile. "They just came out of the oven."

"Perfect," my grandfather said as he grabbed the bag.

When we reached the register, a woman named Mary rang up our order. "Oh, you got some nice warm ones here," she said. "You kids know what you have to do, right?

We all looked confused, but Pop winked, assuring her that he knew. We didn't know what they were talking about, but we soon found out. The plan was to eat them warm. As soon as we got in the car, Pop handed everyone a roll and said, "Enjoy."

It was the best roll I had ever eaten and I could've eaten the whole bag.

"Pop, how did you find this place?" I asked.

"Oh, your grandmother is a bread connoisseur," he laughed. "We found Italian People's many, many years ago."

Luckily, we were going to the College of New Jersey next. At least this would give us an opportunity to walk off all the bread before hitting Marsilio's Kitchen. As we neared the college, we all noticed something at the same time. NJM headquarters were on our left.

"Hey, isn't that…" asked T-Bone.

"Yeah, that's NJM," I interrupted. "It's huge."

"That's their headquarters," Pop explained, "that's where it all began. It's actually a beautiful campus."

"Maybe we should stop in and get those safety tips from Theresa," said T-Bone.

"Or, we should wait for her to send them when they're ready," said Wanda, rolling her eyes.

A few minutes later, we were passing a bunch of stores and apartment buildings as we turned into the main entrance to The College of New Jersey.

"That's Campus Town," said Wanda. "It wasn't here when my mom went to school, but it has stores, restaurants, a gym, an urgent care, and apartments."

"Pretty nice," I said. "I could see myself coming here."

"That settles it," said T-Bone. "We'll all come here."

Pop laughed. "You've literally been on campus for six seconds and you've already decided you want to come here?"

We parked in the visitor's lot facing Trenton Hall and Wanda began her tour. We checked out the student center and the Traditions restaurant, some of the academic buildings, and then the dorms. It always seemed so strange that college students were allowed to come and go as they pleased.

When a group of students walked by, T-Bone didn't hesitate to ask them if they liked living at college.

"Sure," said a boy carrying his skateboard and a backpack. "It's a great campus. You should stop by Eick before you leave."

"And, definitely check out the sports facilities," said one of the girls. "I play softball and our stadium is really nice."

"Definitely," said Wanda. "How are the dorms?"

"They're always building lots of new buildings and dorms, so I'd say pretty good," said another student. "You should stop by Trenton Hall and see if a Griffin could give you a tour."

"Tour guide birds?" T-Bone gasped. "That's incredible. Should we assume that like parrots, these birds speak?"

"Dude, they're not real birds," said the skateboarder. "They're people who mentor students and give tours. Anyway, good luck. We're heading to Eick."

"Oh, I knew that," T-Bone said, his face turning a bright shade of tomato. "I was just joking."

We walked near the library and sat at the tables outside. A girl walked by and hollered to two other girls, "Eick at 4:00, right?" The other two girls nodded.

"Who's Ike? He's seems popular. He must be the big man on campus because everyone's talking about him," said T-Bone. "I'm asking the next person that walks by. I wanna meet him."

Before Wanda could answer his question, he sprang out of his seat and approached a woman walking at a pretty brisk clip.

"Excuse me, wow, you sure walk fast, excuse me," T-Bone said as he started to pant.

"Can I help you?" she asked.

"Actually, yes," said T-Bone, "I'm trying to find Ike."

"Right behind you," the woman said with a smile.

T-Bone turned around to see no one was right behind him.

"Very funny," he said. "But could you please tell me where I could find Ike?"

"Right behind you," she repeated, then smiled and pointed.

"Hold on, I might need glasses," he said. "Because I'm clearly not seeing what you're seeing. Unless you're actually the one who needs glasses. How has your vision been lately?"

"Hi," Wanda interrupted, "please excuse my friend. I was about to tell him that Eick is short for Eickoff which is the dining hall named after a former president."

"Wanda, there was no US President named Eickoff," he said. "Trust me, I have a deck of president cards."

"He's a former president of the college," the woman said.

"Ohhh," T-Bone said slowly. "You meant the building."

"Indeed, I was," she nodded. "Are you prospective students?"

"Kinda," said T-Bone. "That's Wanda and her mom is a lumbar. And we might go here when we finish high school, which we're just about to start."

"So, my mom is an alum," Wanda corrected. "She graduated when this was Trenton State College."

"Nice to meet you, Wanda," said the woman. "I'm actually the president of the college."

"I thought Ike was the president," said T-Bone.

"Dr. Eikoff was the president," she said with a smile. "This building behind you is the dining hall named after him, but we call it Eick."

"That's cool," said T-Bone. "Where's your building?"

"I work over there in Green Hall," she said pointing over his shoulder.

"If you're the president," he continued, "you must be Madame President Green?"

"I don't think they name a building after you when you're still working," said Wanda.

"Oh, like the Hall of Fame," said T-Bone. "You have to wait until you retire to get inducted."

"Something like that," she said. "Since you're here, would you like to check Eick out for yourself?"

We followed her inside and it was the exact opposite of what I had envisioned. It was more like Epcot than a school dining hall. It was bright and colorful and there were so many different food stations. I wondered how students decided what to eat each day. There was a grill, a deli, a salad bar, a Mexican station, a Chinese station, sushi, breakfast, entrees and side dishes, desserts, and even a soft ice cream machine.

“Can I just live here?” I asked in complete and total awe. “Like, seriously, in this booth right here?”

“Good news,” she said, "you don’t have to live in a booth. This is also a dorm so you could live above the dining hall.”

“Close enough,” I said.

“As the president, I should probably inform you that we have many more reasons to attend TCNJ besides the ice cream.”

“Madame President,” said T-Bone. “Please, convince Wanda, I mean, um, all of us, why we should all go here.”

“Well,” she began, “TCNJ is known for its natural beauty. We’re situated on 289 tree-lined acres, with a strong liberal arts core and a wealth of degree programs offered through the college’s seven schools: Arts and Communication, Business, Education, Engineering, Humanities and Social Sciences, Nursing, Health, and Exercise Science, and Science.”

“Stop,” said T-Bone. “That’s all wrong. It sounds like something in a brochure. It’s flat and boring, like background noise. Now, try again, but this time really sell it.”

She stopped for a moment, then nodded. I had no idea what she would say next. Would she decide that she had about enough of T-Bone or go along with his request that she sell him on the idea of attending the college for which she’s the president. My money was on her politely excusing herself or pretending she was getting a phone call.

"What are you thinking? Like an elevator pitch?" she asked.

"Oh, I've seen those on business shows," said T-Bone. "You have to pitch your idea in a minute while wearing a suit and standing in an elevator. Unfortunately, I don't have a suit or an elevator handy."

The president laughed and told T-Bone he didn't need a suit or an elevator. He seemed relieved. Then she began.

"Okay, my elevator pitch as to why you should apply to The College of New Jersey. *New Jersey has a variety of colleges and universities in a variety of sizes and a variety of settings. The College of New Jersey provides a world class education on a beautiful campus. Our faculty and staff go above and beyond for our students, and you can make lifelong friendships. But the biggest reason to apply is the opportunity to keep learning while you prepare yourself for your future.* How'd I do?"

"You must ride a lot of elevators," said T-Bone, "because you convinced me. How about you Wanda? Did she convince you? Please say she convinced you."

"I think about my future a lot," said Wanda, "and I always seem to picture myself attending TCNJ. Part of it is because my mom went here and brings us on campus frequently and the other part is everything you just shared. I always felt like this is the perfect sized campus for me."

"That settles it," said T-Bone. "It's official. It looks like we'll see you in four years."

"Oh, one more thing," she added, "while our dining halls are definitely amazing, we also have cookie deliveries until 3:00 am."

"What?" T-Bone shrieked. "Who eats cookies at 3:00 am?"

"Once you've pulled an all-nighter, you'll understand the need for after-hours cookies," said Pop.

"Well, I'm impressed," said T-Bone.

"Glad you're impressed," she said. "See you in four years."

"Count on it," said T-Bone.

We said good-bye and did exactly what she suggested. T-Bone even saw a few students having fun and throwing a frisbee. He immediately jumped in the game. Unfortunately, he never played with a frisbee or watched a real frisbee game. He had only seen the dog food commercials with the dogs catching frisbees. The only difference was that dogs use their mouths to catch frisbees.

"Over here, over here," yelled T-Bone, waving his arms as if he knew what he was doing. "Over here!"

He caught the attention of the girl who was about to throw the frisbee. Hearing him yell, she quickly turned and threw it to T-Bone. And that's when it happened. As a perfect throw was heading his way, he dropped his arms and opened his mouth as wide as he could. The entire group of students suddenly stopped and opened their mouths in horror. I remember yelling,

"Use your hands!" and T-Bone turning to say, "What?"

That's when the situation took a weird turn. The frisbee plowed right into the side of T-Bone's head.

"Hey, are you alright," asked a guy wearing a bucket hat.

T-Bone stood there, somewhat in shock, rubbing his head.

"Dude, what were you thinking?" asked one of the guys.

"Every dog in the world catches a frisbee with their mouth?" T-Bone responded. "I've seen the dog food commercials."

"They don't have hands," said a girl with curly hair as she looked in her backpack for a band-aid.

"You might want to ice that," said the girl who threw it to him. "You could end up with a pretty big bump."

After a quick examination, Pop decided that it was time to stop by the store and then head to the restaurant. Marsilio's Kitchen was only a few minutes from campus and as soon as we walked in, I knew what Italy must smell like.

"Well, the gang's all here," said Alan as he approached us.

"All present, accounted for, and starving," said Pop.

"I saved you a table," said Alan Meinster. A moment later, he introduced us to his wife, Denise, and his daughter, Grace.

"So, you're the ambassadors?" Denise said with a smile. "He told me all about you after your visit to Rossi's."

"That's us," said T-Bone. "Although we're still unofficial."

"Well, we're officially happy to have you here," said Grace.

"So, we learned a lot about Rossi's history," said Wanda. "Can you tell us a little about Marsilio's history?"

"Sure," said Alan. "The original owner, Marzillio, opened it in 1951. I started working in restaurants when I was 15-years-old and after years of working as a waiter, a dishwasher, and a cook, I became the chef. When I was 31-years-old, I decided I wanted to own the restaurant."

"That sounds scary," I said. "And 31 seems pretty young."

"I was definitely young," Alan agreed, "but I had Denise and my mother-in-law, Grace, on my side. In fact, my mother-in-law bought it with me. That was the original location on Roebling Avenue in Trenton."

"Wow, she must've really liked you," I said. "And it looks like she made the right decision."

"That's so interesting," said Wanda. "I always wonder how family businesses are created. It's great to meet the people who took a chance on starting their own business."

"It can definitely be scary," said Denise. "But it's worth it."

"I hope you're hungry," said Grace. "My dad has some special platters prepared so you can sample different options."

"Let the games begin," said T-Bone. "Unless that game is frisbee, then I'm out."

"Does that explain the frisbee shaped lump on your head?" asked Alan.

"Yup," T-Bone nodded. "But don't worry, I learned my lesson. I'll never turn my head when a frisbee comes my way again."

"Nothing about catching it with your hands instead of your mouth?" I asked.

"You didn't?" asked Grace as she started to laugh. "You tried to catch it with your mouth?"

"I'm still confused," said T-Bone. "Have dogs been doing it wrong all this time?"

Before anyone could answer, our server Sandra brought over baskets of warm bread and butter and a couple of platters. Pop told Alan everything was outstanding, and we all nodded. We were too busy eating to talk. There were giant meatballs, garlic bread and calamari, followed by a giant bowl of salad. When Sandra came over to take our order, I thought she was giving Pop the check.

"There's more?" I asked.

"It's just the beginning," said Denise as she handed us menus. While Sandra took Pop's order, I changed my mind twelve times. Everything sounded so good. I couldn't decide between lasagna, vodka rigatoni, or fettuccini alfredo. Then I saw the chicken section. Then I saw an entrée created for me. It was in the *I Can't Decide* section and there was a dish called *Everything Parm.* It was chicken parm, eggplant parm, and meatball parm.

Denise heard my order and said, "I created that section because I can never decide."

"Good thinking," I agreed. "Finally, a restaurant that gets me."

Our meal was incredible and Alan, Denise, and Grace stopped by frequently to check on us and catch up with Pop. When Denise asked me what I thought about my Everything Parm meal, I told her they should call it *Everything Perfect* instead. Then, just when I was about to wave the white flag, Grace brought out a platter called *I Can't Decide Dessert.* Clearly, this was the perfect dessert for T-Bone.

"You know, if we all go to TCNJ, we could come here for some of our meals," said T-Bone. "And our desserts."

"Actually, Alan and I went to TCNJ when it was still Trenton State College," said Denise. "And then we got married."

"Really?" asked T-Bone as he winked at Wanda. "You went to college together and then got married? That's good to know. Very, very good to know."

Chapter Nine

What's Your Dalmation Situation?

The next morning, I woke up filled with regret. Why did I eat everything last night? I wished I would have brought some home for today. It was so good, though, I couldn't stop. Next time, I would definitely have more self-control.

"How was your night?" asked my mom. "I must have fallen asleep before you got home."

I told her all about our day, from Italian People's Bakery to The College of New Jersey to Marsilio's Kitchen. I loved how so many of the restaurants we visited were family businesses. They were my favorite types of restaurants. Places like Pete's Steakhouse, DeLorenzo's, Rossi's, and Marsilio's Kitchen had so much history. They had all been passed down from older generations and, of course, the food was outstanding.

"So, Eddie called for you," she said. He said to tell you he arranged for you to visit the Vineland and Union Township Fire Departments."

"Really?" I asked. "That's awesome. He sure gets stuff done quick."

"He's a firefighter," said my mom. "I don't think they have any other speed."

"True," I agreed. "Slow firefighters definitely wouldn't be too helpful."

I returned Eddie's call and we set up both trips. My next two calls would have been Wanda and T-Bone, but they were at my door before I could finish dialing.

"I'm still stuffed," said T-Bone. "I should have saved some to bring home for today. I really need to start working on my self-control."

"Me, too," I laughed. "Me, too."

"Should we call Eddie and set up the remaining fire department visits?" asked Wanda.

"Already done," I said. "Although maybe we should look up some background information for both locations."

"Already done," she said. "I have it right here."

"Well, these firefighters should have it much easier than Atlantic City, since they don't have the Ocean, the boardwalk, and all of those huge casinos and hotels," said T-Bone. "And it should definitely be easier than a capital city like Trenton."

"I don't think it works that way," I said. "Even though Trenton doesn't have an ocean or giant casinos and hotels, it's extremely difficult to be a firefighter there."

"That's because Trenton has the Capitol Complex with all of the state buildings, a river, and a lot of very old homes," said T-Bone. "I don't think Vineland or Union Township could be that difficult at all. It's probably super boring."

"Just because they have different challenges doesn't mean they have it easy," said Wanda. "I'm sure they're all very difficult."

"I don't know," said T-Bone. "I'm thinking Vineland will have a hammock in the firehouse. They may even have a game room and massage chairs like at the mall. Should I bring quarters?"

Luckily, we wouldn't have to wait long to find out. Our Vineland trip was the next morning and my dad offered to drive. We reviewed Wanda's background information and learned a lot of interesting facts about Vineland. For instance, Wanda read that it's considered a rural city. I had never even heard that term before and almost didn't believe her, but it was true. Vineland was a city with 60,000 people but was also home to some of the state's most important agriculture. Farms, clearly, were not a major feature of most New Jersey cities. I continued to read.

"Wow, " I said. "The Welch's company was started in Vineland. Thomas Bramwell Welch and his son, Charles started it."

"We should try to meet them," said T-Bone. "That way I can thank them for my favorite sandwich."

"Peanut butter and jelly?" asked Wanda.

"Nope," he shook his head. "Jelly."

"What does that mean?" I asked. "Just jelly?"

"Just jelly?" he asked. "Grape jelly and strawberry jelly together. It's amazing. I guess you could say jelly is my jam. Get it? Jelly is my jam. I'm cracking myself up."

"Got it," I said.

"Are you sure?" he asked. "Because you're not laughing."

"That's because it isn't funny," said Wanda.

"Agree to disagree," said Pop. "That one wasn't too bad."

"Anyway," T-Bone continued. "I really should thank them for jellying two of my favorite fruits."

"Well, you might need a time machine," I laughed.

"Why?" asked T-Bone. "Have they somehow traveled to the future? I knew it. I knew time travel was real. What year are they in? 2121? 3000? Will cars fly? Will I fly? What new jelly developments can we expect?"

"No, they didn't travel to the future," I said. "They founded Welch's in Vineland back in 1869."

"1869?" T-Bone shrieked. "That might be a problem."

The next morning, we headed down Route 206. My dad liked to take the scenic route whenever he could. As we reached Hammonton, we could tell we were in a city. This city, however, was different than so many New Jersey cities. There was a main street, lots of businesses, and even a toy store. When we approached a big intersection, the train crossing lights started blinking and we waited for a surface level train to pass. We passed another stretch of businesses and then something caught my eye.

"Hey, there's another NJM Insurance building," I said as we approached.

"This is their South Jersey hub," said Pop.

"It looks like offices," said T-Bone, "which makes sense, since they're not actually manufacturing insurance in a factory."

"That's because no one makes insurance in a factory," Pop laughed. "Remember, they protect things like your life, your health, and your property."

"They should make bad grade insurance," said T-Bone.

"They do," Wanda sighed. "It's called studying."

As we left Hammonton, we made a couple of turns and pulled up in front of Vineland Fire Department Headquarters. Funny, I thought as we entered. I didn't see anyone in a hammock or in massage chairs playing video games. I didn't see a dalmatian or smell chili on the stove. T-Bone was wrong again. I hated to admit it, but it never got old.

Captain Mike Feaster greeted us. "Welcome to Vineland and welcome to the Vineland Fire Headquarters. Actually, welcome to the old Fire Headquarters."

"Do you have a new one?" asked T-Bone.

"We will soon," he said. "This one is 45-years-old and has six engine bays. The new one will be twice as big and will have 12 engine bays."

"Wow, that sounds huge," I said. "How many trucks do you have at headquarters?"

"Right now, we house an Engine, a Ladder Tower, a Rescue truck, and a Recon truck," he explained.

"You must be excited," said T-Bone. "I remember how excited I was when I got a new toy firehouse for Christmas. Well, until my brother sat on it and crushed it."

"Do us a favor and keep your brother away from our new house," Mike laughed.

"So, Captain Feaster, would you mind if we asked you some questions?" said Wanda.

"Of course," he said. "And call me Mike."

"Thank you, Mike," she replied. "What do you consider to be the fire department's biggest role?"

"I'd say that we believe our biggest role is to protect lives and property and to be involved in the community we serve," he answered. "I'm not sure if you're aware of this, but we're a hybrid department."

"Your trucks use gas and electric?" asked T-Bone. "Are the electric trucks super quiet? Are they so quiet that you can sneak up on people when you drive under 5 miles per hour?"

"No," Mike laughed. "Fire trucks aren't very stealth, and we've never been accused of sneaking up on anyone. They're pretty loud and that's before the lights and sirens. Hybrid means we're a mix of volunteer and career firefighters."

"You have both?" asked T-Bone.

"Sure," he said, "We have about 120 volunteer firefighters and 33 career firefighters."

"Why not have all volunteers?" I asked.

"That's a good question," said another firefighter. "Hi, I'm Captain John Hendershot and this is Firefighter Matt Haught.

You know, most departments began as all volunteer."

"Seems cheaper," I said.

"Well, cheaper in some ways," said John. "Less money for salaries, sure, but more money spent on loss of property and loss of life. Volunteers are amazing individuals, risking their lives for no compensation, but it takes time to have them come from their homes and jobs."

"Those valuable minutes can sometimes mean the difference between a small fire or a five alarm fire," said Matt. "Or also the difference between life and death."

"So, you have some of both?" I asked. "Sounds smart."

"We're lucky to have so many dedicated individuals willing to risk their lives," said Mike. "You know, we're a very big fire district, roughly 70 square miles."

"Wow," said Wanda. "That's almost 10 times as big as Trenton."

"Vineland is pretty unique," said John. "We are a city surrounded by rural farmlands and industrial areas as well as some of the highest poverty levels in the state."

"That sounds like quite a challenge," said Wanda.

"It is," said Matt. "That's why we're all universally trained. Each member of our department must be trained for everything. We have this station and five volunteer stations."

"Interesting," said T-Bone. "But, what's your chili and dalmatian situation like?"

"Our chili and dalmatian situation?" asked John.

"I'm just curious how a hybrid department handles the chili cookoffs and the dalmatian walking," T-Bone continued. "It must be a scheduling nightmare."

They all seemed confused, so they just started the tour. They told us about the city's original professional equipment: *buckets.* The stories of the human chain bucket brigade, including women and children, were riveting. When a man named C.B. Bagster tried to convince residents to upgrade their firefighting capabilities, people rejected his ideas. It turns out fire is one of those things people only think about when something's on fire. And that's exactly what changed people's minds. On July 22, 1867, a fire roared out of control, destroying buildings and businesses. It was only stopped when the wooden grocery store was knocked down to stop the fire from spreading to the mechanics block. This finally convinced people to move forward with conveniently placed extinguishers, apparatus, and companies to operate them.

"It's hard to imagine a community without a fire department," I said. "We're so used to having firehouses, fire trucks, and firefighters, it's easy to forget that this wasn't always a thing."

"I agree," said Matt. "And each town has its own unique story of how their fire department was founded. If you go to our website, you can read all about Vineland's story."

"I guess you never get bored," I said, hoping T-Bone wouldn't start talking about video games and kittens in trees.

"We get tired, we get hungry, we get stressed, but we never get bored on the job," said Mike. "And honestly, hands down, this is the best job in the world. Every day you get to help the public in one way or another. And every day is different. Some days you're fighting a fire, some days you're cutting people out of a car, and other days it might be a technical or water rescue. But every shift, we show up to help others."

"When do you play video games and make chili?" asked T-Bone. "There's probably so much time in between calls that you have to entertain yourself. Do you have carnival hour?"

"Entertain ourselves?" Mike laughed. "Oh, we have so many ways of entertaining ourselves. There's cleaning the house, washing trucks, organizing tools, and cooking meals. Then there's drill school, community outreach, and fire prevention. And to answer your question, no, there's no carnival hour."

"Don't forget the reports," said John. "We write a detailed report for every response."

"That doesn't sound very entertaining," said T-Bone.

"Entertaining? No," said Mike. "Satisfying? Exhausting? Rewarding? Absolutely."

"What would you tell the kids that read our reports?" I asked.

Mike began. "I'd say if you think there's an emergency, call it in. Call 9-1-1. We never get upset if someone thinks there may be an emergency and it turns out it wasn't. Sometimes, by the time you determine if something is serious, we could have taken care of it by then. Instead, when people wait, things can get out of control. So, if you see something, say something."

They showed us pictures of the other Vineland firehouses and then showed us fire district maps. Vineland really was huge. It seemed like an enormous responsibility. Even with 10 Engines, 5 Ladders, 1 Rescue truck, and 3 Brush trucks, it still seemed difficult to cover almost 70 square miles. Mike said that the low number of career firefighters and a decline in volunteers meant they were always trying to do more with less.

Before we left, I saw T-Bone scanning the building. "What are you doing?" I asked.

"Just checking for hammocks," he said. "I don't see any hammocks or smell any chili, so I guess they really are pretty busy. When we visit Union Township, they'll probably have the whole leisure and recreation vibe."

I ignored him. Some things T-Bone had to learn for himself. We thanked everyone for taking the time to meet with us and promised to share all their tips with our readers. On the drive home, we passed by NJM, continued through Hammonton, then made a right on Route 30.

"This isn't the way home," I said to my dad, pretty proud that I recognized he was making a mistake.

He ignored me and kept driving. "Maybe he didn't hear you," T-Bone texted me. "Should I yell, *you're wrong* in his ear?"

"No!" I texted back. "Are you crazy?"

Before I knew it, we were pulling into Joe Italiano's Maplewood Restaurant. I remembered this restaurant from our previous adventures. This was definitely a surprise. Joe's homemade food was legendary, and we were starving.

"Thought I was going home the wrong way?" asked my dad.

"Dad, are we eating here or bringing dinner home?" I asked.

"I spoke to your mom, and she said they ate already so we should stop and get dinner," he replied.

"I don't know if this is a good idea," I said. "You know, Maggie really likes Italian food."

"That's true," said my dad, "but there's a simple solution."

"What's that?" I asked.

"Enjoy your dinner, but do not, under any circumstances," he began, "get anything on your shirt."

Chapter Ten

I'm Basically Here For The Chili

"Nick, are you coming?" T-Bone asked from the hallway outside my bedroom.

"Coming where?" I asked.

"To Union Township to visit the fire department," he replied. "You're late."

"We're going to Union Township today?" I asked. "No one mentioned this to me."

"Yeah, about that," he began, "I meant to tell you yesterday and totally forgot. Then I meant to call you this morning, but my mom was about to serve breakfast. You should have seen the size of these pancakes. They were as big as the plate. In fact, I might start calling them platecakes. Anyway, then I ran over here and caught breakfast with your parents and sisters."

"So, at no point during your multiple breakfasts did it cross your mind to tell me?" I asked.

"It did cross my mind," he admitted, "but it just didn't stick."

"What time are we leaving?" I asked.

"Oh yeah, about that," he hesitated. "We're leaving in just about approximately five minutes ago."

Leave it to T-Bone to arrive at my house early, sit down for a meal, and still forget to tell me about it. By the time he told me about it, we were already late. I jumped in the shower and got ready as quick as I could. It turned out my dad was bringing us again, along with Timmy, Maggie, and Emma.

"Nicky, what took you so long?" asked Maggie with her hands on her hips and her foot tapping.

"Someone forgot to tell me we were going today," I replied as I turned toward T-Bone.

"T-Bone, it was you, wasn't it?" Maggie demanded. "Really, T-Bone?"

"Don't forget the cooler of water bottles and snacks I packed for you," my mom interrupted. "And be careful that you don't get too much sun."

"Are we going to the beach, too?" asked Maggie. "Because if we are, you should remind T-Bone not to leave the lid open."

"No," said my mom. "You're not going to the beach, and I think the seagulls taught T-Bone that lesson years ago."

"It wouldn't hurt to remind him," Maggie continued.

My mom called Maggie over for a one-on-one about her attitude and then gave her the look. It was a shame my dad didn't have the look. My mom was a teacher, so it came natural to her. My poor dad would just yell at us.

We headed toward the turnpike and proceeded north. Before we knew it, we were in Union Township in Union County. My dad pulled up to the firehouse and Maggie and Emma began to immediately cheer.

"Show us the dogs," said Emma. "I wanna pet the dogs. Do they keep all 101 dalmatians, at this firehouse?"

"And I want to drive the fire truck," said Maggie. "Will they let me drive on the street or do I have to stay in the parking lot?"

"I'm basically here for the chili," said Timmy. "I even put some bread in the cooler in case it's real five alarm chili. You know when you eat really spicy food, you should eat bread, not drink water. Water makes it worse."

My dad turned off the car and said, "What are you guys talking about? They don't have 101 dalmatians here. And Maggie you aren't driving a fire truck. You're a kid. And Timmy, they don't just keep a pot of chili on for visitors. Where would you kids get these crazy ideas?"

"T-Bone," they all said at the same time.

"In my defense," he began, "I didn't say for sure. I said maybe they would have dalmatians and maybe you can sit in the driver's seat and maybe they'll have chili."

At that moment, my dad was probably asking himself why he volunteered to bring six kids to Union Township.

"I've got this, Mr. A.," said Wanda. "Emma, they'll probably give you a coloring book that has pictures of dalmatians and a bright red fire hat that you can keep. Maggie, they'll probably let you sit in the driver's seat and maybe even turn on the lights or the siren, but adults can't even drive those trucks unless they're actually firefighters. And Timmy, maybe just ask if they ever enter any chili contests."

Well done, I thought. Wanda either had a bright future as a teacher or as a hostage negotiator. She was calm under pressure and knew what would do the trick with each person. My mom would have been proud, my dad was just grateful.

Eddie greeted us at the door and immediately started telling us about Union Township and the fire department. When another firefighter, Bill Brower, mentioned Union County, T-Bone interrupted him and said, "I'm sorry, but you said the wrong county. This is Hunterdon County."

"Nope," said Eddie. "This is Union County."

"Wow, this is going to be embarrassing for you," said T-Bone, "but if I don't correct you, you'll keep making the same mistake. This is Hunterdon County."

"Actually," said Bill, "a lot of people make that mistake. This is Union Township in Union County. This is one of the four Unions in New Jersey."

"We have four places in New Jersey named Union?" T-Bone gasped. "Seriously? Isn't that a bit confusing?"

"Well, there's Union Township in Union County, Union City in Hudson County, Union Township in Hunterdon County, and Union Beach Boro in Monmouth County," said firefighter, Matthew Howard. "Five if you include the County of Union."

"That is extremely confusing," T-Bone sighed. "Whose idea was that anyway?"

"Not really sure," said Bill. "But I guess we're just used to it."

"Tell us about your Union Township," said Wanda.

"Well, as we mentioned, we're the Union Township of Union County," said Eddie. "Our township is about 9 square miles, and our population is approximately 58,000 people."

"How does that compare to the other Unions?" asked T-Bone. "Are you in the lead?"

"I don't really know what you mean since its not a competition," said Matthew, "but the Union Township in Hunterdon is about 20 square miles and has almost 6,000 people. Union Beach Boro is a little less than 2 square miles and has a little over 5,000 people and Union City in Hudson County has an area of a little over a square mile with almost 70,000 people."

"Wow, the biggest land area has the fewest people," said T-Bone. "And Union City in Hudson has 70,000 people squished into a little over a square mile?"

"There's a reason we're the densest state in the country," said Wanda. "We have more people per square mile than India."

"Interesting," said T-Bone.

"I guess in comparison, our township is in the middle of the Unions," said Bill.

"Can't win them all," said T-Bone. "Maybe if you put in a few water parks, more people will move here."

"It's not a competition," I whispered as I nudged him and gave him my mom's look.

"Anyway," said Eddie, "our town is pretty diverse and has an abundance of homes, commercial structures, highways, a train station, and even Kean College."

"That seems like a lot to protect," I said. "Except for highways. I mean, it's not like a highway will just burst into flames."

"You're right," said Matt. "Highways don't generally burst into flames, but cars do. We put out vehicle fires, we extricate people who are trapped in vehicles, and we clean up chemical spills."

"That's right," said Eddie. "Our district includes parts of the very busy Garden State Parkway and Routes 78 and 22."

"I would think the vehicle incidents alone would keep you super busy," said Wanda. "Do you have any advice to reduce the number of motor vehicle accidents?"

"We do," said Bill. "Don't text and drive. We see people driving with their heads down all the time. Don't do it. There is nothing at all in that message that's worth your life or worth killing someone else. If something is that important, pull over in a safe place and text there. Honestly, we see the results of distracted driving, speeding, and your everyday recklessness each shift."

"The results?" asked T-Bone as he gulped.

"Absolutely," said Matt. "We see people who are severely injured and sometimes we even need to close the road to allow a helicopter to airlift a patient. Then there are the people who don't survive the accident and it's truly heartbreaking. Someone's just driving somewhere and suddenly, because of their actions or the actions of someone else, they never arrive at their destination."

"Please say that's because it would bring back too many bad memories to return," said T-Bone.

"No," said Eddie, turning serious. "That's because they didn't survive and they become another fatality."

I couldn't imagine responding to such tragedies, shift after shift. Firefighting was so much more than fighting fire. I wanted to find a tactful way to ask them why they did it. Why they risked their lives to save the lives and property of people they didn't even know. Why they ran toward danger when everyone else was running away. Why they sacrificed sleep and holidays with their own families, missing events, and big moments to save strangers. While I struggled to find a polite way to ask, T-Bone didn't hesitate.

"If you don't mind me asking," said T-Bone, "why do you do this job? It's dangerous, stressful, and probably unhealthy with all the smoke and chemicals you inhale. And apparently firehouses don't even make a pot of chili every day. Or, have hammocks and puppies. So, why would you do that? Why not find a nice, safe desk job?"

"Honestly," said Eddie, "that's a good question. It must seem strange to you, but it's the best job in the world. It's an honor and a privilege to serve the community and impact someone in a positive way during a difficult or tragic time in their lives. Sure, it's physically and emotionally demanding and mentally challenging and there's a lot of stress both on and off the job, but we have the opportunity to do good things every day. That's why we do it."

"He's right," said Bill, "Of course, we make critical decisions that can ultimately impact a life-or-death situation, but we train every day for those moments. Which is why we don't have time for dalmatians and random chili cookoffs."

"Although we do love chili and dogs," said Eddie.

"Throughout our careers," added Matt, "we experience and are exposed to so many things most people will never see in their entire lifetime. But in their own time of crisis, people look to us to solve the problem, to save them, to provide security. For firefighters, it's not just a job, it's our life."

"Is that why we always see stories on the news about off-duty firefighters saving people?" asked Wanda.

"Exactly," said Eddie. "Firefighters are never really off-duty. If there's an emergency, whether we're on duty or off duty, we respond. That's why we're like family; it's in our blood. It's how we're wired."

"You know what I always tell people?" said Billy. "I've never worked a day in my life, I'm just living my kindergarten dream."

"Wow," said Wanda. "You guys are really inspiring."

"I just hope my kindergarten dream doesn't come true one day," said T-Bone.

"What was your dream?" I asked.

"I wanted to be a fire truck," said T-Bone. "I wanted to be *Tommy the Fire Truck*."

"You wanted to be the *truck*?" I asked. "The actual truck?"

"Yup," he nodded. "Except I wanted to be the fire truck with the really long ladder and big tires."

"That's definitely a new twist," said Matt. "And you're in luck. Since a fire truck can weigh 50,000 pounds, they all have really big tires."

"You all seem to love your job," I said. "Do you have advice for kids who may want to follow in your footsteps?"

"Absolutely," said Bill. "Work hard, harder than you think you have to. Dream big, bigger than you think you should. And never, ever, let anyone or anything get in the way of your dream."

"That's great advice," I said. "Thank you."

"Any time," said Bill. "Now, let's give you a tour."

The tour was interesting and I noticed more than the actual firehouse and equipment. Watching the firefighters, it was clear that the department really becomes their second family. They live in the same house, eat in the same kitchen, sleep in the same bunk rooms, and they always have each other's backs. The way that they relied on each other was probably the most obvious and most important thing that we noticed.

Eddie definitely knew what he was doing when he suggested we visit a variety of firehouses. We learned so much during each visit. Despite unique challenges and different resources, the one thing every department had in common is that when a call came in, a highly trained department would respond.

"So, Sirloin," Eddie said to T-Bone with a smile, "should we expect your job application in a few years?"

"I'd love to," he said, "and I'm not scared at all. It's just my meal-times might not be flexible enough for this line of work. You understand, right?"

"Absolutely," he laughed. "This line of work is definitely not for everyone. And you never know, you may change your mind one day."

"I don't know," said T-Bone. "I like to eat on schedule, sleep through the night, and most importantly, I usually run away from danger. I once took a fight or flight quiz and…"

"Let me guess," said Eddie. "Flight?"

"Oh, it was flight alright," said T-Bone. "So, I guess that doesn't make me a good firefighter candidate, does it?"

"At your age, we completely recommend flight," said Eddie. "In fact, flight is often the best response for everything, depending upon the situation. You may see us rush toward danger, but it's very thoughtful and planned out."

Eddie was right. We really had no idea where we would end up in the future. Some people even change their career in their 40s and 50s. I recently saw a grandfather graduate from college at 75 years old. In life anything was possible, and I liked to think firefighting could possibly be in my future. Plus, unlike T-Bone, *I could eat dinner at any time.*

Chapter Eleven

The Top Banana

Between the Trenton, Atlantic City, Vineland, and Union Township fire departments, I felt extremely confident in my knowledge of community firefighting. Thanks to Quincy at the New Jersey Forest Fire Service, I felt just as confident in my knowledge of forest fires. With so much information, we decided to break our report down into three categories. I focused on prevention, Wanda focused on what to do in an emergency, and T-Bone focused on careers in the fire service. Shockingly, it was all coming together nicely.

As I was going over our notes, an email from Paul at NJM came in. She had put together a list of fire prevention tips and general safety tips for us. Perfect timing, I thought. For the next hour, we were completely silent as we compiled our information.

"Okay, listen to this," I said. "Here's what I have so far for fire prevention. Number one, extension cords. Never use frayed or old cords, never place them under a rug, never overload them, and never connect multiple cords to each other."

"Good," said Wanda. "People probably think that tucking an extension cord under a rug simply prevents a tripping hazard when they're actually creating a fire hazard."

"Exactly," I continued. "Second, never play with matches or lighters and if you see them sitting out, grab them and place them out of the reach of kids."

"Very important," she agreed. "Curious kids and lighters are a dangerous combination."

"Third, never leave a stove unattended or you may end up with a culinary mishap," I added. "And never let young kids near the stove or oven."

"Speaking of young kids," said T-Bone, "what about keeping all medicines and cleaning products out of the reach of kids. I know it's not actual fire, but it's definitely important."

"That's a good point," said Wanda. "Each firehouse we visited reminded us that firefighters don't just fight fires. They respond to so many different kinds of emergency situations."

"I honestly don't know how they can be prepared to respond to every possible thing that could happen," said T-Bone. "And I definitely didn't realize they respond to emergency medical calls. They're like the firefighter-hero-paramedic-car-rescue-chemical-spill guys."

"Wait, what? You're admitting that firefighting isn't hyped up for Hollywood?" I asked.

"I am," said T-Bone. "I stand corrected. Firefighting is definitely for special, brave, selfless people who can eat any time of the day. Although they should try to stretch more."

"It's about time," said Wanda, shaking her head. "By the way, Nick, did you include vehicle safety?"

"Yup," I said as I flipped through my work. "Let's see, there's the obvious things like always wear your seatbelt, never, ever drink and drive, and make sure all kids are in appropriate car seats and booster seats. Then I added what the firefighters in Union Township told us about distracted driving."

"Good point," said Wanda. "Distracted driving is much more than texting. It can be talking or texting on a phone, eating, or hollering at kids in the back seat. Either way, it causes a lot of accidents."

"I'm never gonna use my phone and drive," said T-Bone. "It's a pretty stupid way to die. Why can't people just pull over if it's that important?"

"Well, it's like Wayne said," I replied, "no one thinks anything bad will ever happen to them. So many people believe they're invincible."

"Not me," said T-Bone as he shook his head for emphasis. "I assume everything bad will happen to me."

"Well, that's not good either," said Wanda. "You just have to find the balance between believing you're invincible and not living in fear."

"What about speeding?" said T-Bone. "And tailgating? And changing lanes too many times? Those will all get you killed."

"They're definitely dangerous," said my mom as she entered the room, "but good drivers don't just make sure they're driving safely. Good drivers are always aware of who's around them. It's called defensive driving."

"I'd rather do offensive driving," said T-Bone. "You score more points on offense."

"It's not a game," my mom said in her teacher voice. "Offensive drivers break the rules. They're the people good drivers have to watch out for."

"It's okay," I said to my mom. "He has no idea what he's talking about. He was trying to make a sports reference, even though the only sport he follows in Stick Volley on You Tube. He's the same guy who tried to catch a frisbee in his mouth at TCNJ."

"What?" my mom shrieked. "Why would you do that?"

"That's how dogs catch frisbees, T-Bone," said Maggie as she walked in. "Do you think you're a dog, T-Bone? Do you?"

I watched as my mom pulled Maggie in for another one-on-one conversation. She emerged with a fake smile and my mom's eyes on her, and she proceeded to apologize to T-Bone for her rude attitude.

"I forgive you," said T-Bone.

Maggie was just about to give him another sassy reply when my mom gave her another look. She thought better of whatever she was about to say and said, "Thank you, T-Bone."

"Are you going to include changing smoke detector batteries and using carbon monoxide detectors?" asked my mom. "That's such a simple, inexpensive precaution that saves so many lives each year."

"Not only did I include how important they are, but I also included that people could call their local firehouse and get free smoke detectors and installation," I said. "It turns out smoke detectors are an important tool for surviving a fire."

"If people can buy them or have their fire department bring a free one, why doesn't everyone have them?" Timmy asked as he joined us.

"Well, a lot of people have them," said my mom, "but they don't change the batteries twice a year when we change the clocks. Or, even worse, if they need a battery, they take it from the smoke detector and then forget to replace it. It can turn out to be a deadly mistake."

"There's so much information," I said. "That's not even half of mine and we still have to add Wanda and T-Bone's."

"The best advice I can give you is to keep it simple," said my mom. "Short paragraphs or sentences, bullet points, and some graphics are always best."

My mom had a good point. What good was having awesome information if it was so overwhelming, people didn't read it all? We definitely needed to simplify it.

"I've got it," said T-Bone. "Remember that calendar I had that gave you a new word everyday?"

"The word-a-day calendar?" I asked.

"No, I think it had a catchier name," he replied.

"Nope," I continued, "it's definitely the word-a-day calendar."

"Agree to disagree," he said. "Anyway, what if we gave kids a safety-tip-a-day?"

"You want to make a calendar?" I gasped.

"He's actually got a pretty good idea," said Wanda. "What if we created a list that schools could read over the intercom during daily announcements? It's actually kind of brilliant."

He looked at me and said, "See? I'm kind of brilliant." Then he turned to Wanda, "Wait, we're not making a calendar?"

"No, we're not making a calendar," she said. "How would we produce calendars? But a list that schools could use would be easy for everyone. They could just download and print it."

"Not a bad idea," I agreed. "We could even arrange them by date so that cold weather tips were announced during the winter and warm weather tips were announced in early fall and late spring."

"Cold weather tips?" asked T-Bone. "Like what? Button up your coat and wear your mittens? Or, don't hug a snowman."

"I was thinking about telling kids not to go on frozen lakes, ponds, and rivers," I replied. "Sometimes the ice looks really solid and it's not. If you fall through, the current under the water can carry you away from the hole where you entered."

"That's horrifying," said T-Bone, his eyes widening. "Yeah, definitely add that one in there."

"How about not using stoves to warm your house," said Wanda, "or not putting heaters near furniture, walls, or fabrics."

"Exactly," I agreed. "This is good. We'll do all of the tips we're working on, and then make a list with one tip for each day. When this is all completed, we'll post it on the website."

Two hours later, just as we were about to take a break and grab some snacks, Pop walked in carrying a brown bag. We instantly recognized the aroma.

"Is that a bag of rolls from Italian People's Bakery?" I asked.

"You're in luck," said Pop. "I met an old friend in Trenton this morning and figured I'd surprise your grandmother with her favorite bread."

"You in trouble with the Mrs.?" asked T-Bone. "If so, you might want to try flowers."

"No, I'm not in trouble," my grandfather said with a shake of his head. "And trust me, if I was, a bag of Italian People's bread would get me further than all the roses in the world."

"Good to know," said T-Bone. "I'll have to tell my dad for the next time he's in trouble."

"Anyway," Pop changed the subject, "I was wondering if you guys felt like taking a ride to Captain Paul's Firehouse Dogs."

With all this talk about firefighting, that was a perfect idea. We all agreed that we could use a break and figured what was more fitting than a fire safety report break at a firehouse themed restaurant. The best part was that the air was unusually dry with no humidity, so eating outside would be great.

We went inside to order and saw Captain Paul as soon as we walked in. I couldn't tell if he remembered us because T-Bone didn't give him a chance.

"Aye-Aye, Captain," said T-Bone. "In case you forgot, I'm T-Bone and this is Wanda, Nicky, and Pop. We're New Jersey's

Unofficial Junior Ambassadors, and we wrote a report about your restaurant a while back."

"Hi guys," said Paul. "Of course, I remember you. How have you been?"

"Busier than ever," said T-Bone. "And pretty hungry, too."

"What can I get you?" asked Paul.

"I'll take what he's having," T-Bone said as he pointed to a man at the counter.

"This is the TFD," said the man. "A fried hot dog with tater tots, onion petals, peppers and mustard. You can't go wrong."

"Make mine a double then," said T-Bone.

"You want two?" asked Paul.

"Oh no, is that what *make mine a double* means?" asked T-Bone. "I'll just take a single, then."

"I'll take the TCNJ," I said. "Pork roll and bacon with melted cheddar and steak fries sounds amazing."

Pop and Wanda also ordered the TFD while I looked at all the fire items that were proudly displayed. Captain Paul's was dedicated to the men and women associated with emergency services, the military and their families, and all those who volunteer to help others. The maltese cross in the center of the awning was a reminder of the 343 firefighters who lost their lives on 9/11.

The first time we met Paul Tweedly, we learned that he was a retired Captain from the Trenton Fire Department and that this was another great family business. Paul told us that it wasn't just his actual family, but he considered the men and women he served with on the fire department his family, too. The feeling must have been mutual because there were Trenton firefighters eating outside when we arrived. It was reassuring to know that if an emergency occurred, all of the off-duty firefighters would spring into action.

While we waited for our food, T-Bone struck up a conversation with the man at the counter. "So, do you eat here often?"

"Whenever I can," the man said with a smile. He then extended his hand. "I'm Rich Mikutsky. I'm the State Fire Marshall."

"Wait, what?" asked T-Bone as though he was just introduced to a King. "You're the top banana? The big dog? The Grand Poobah of New Jersey Firefighters?"

He smiled and said, "I don't know about all of that, but I am in charge of New Jersey's Fire Service."

T-Bone just stared at him. When it started to get awkward, Wanda and I introduced ourselves. "Don't worry," I explained. "He gets like this whenever he meets important people."

"It's true," said Wanda. "He froze when he met the Cake Boss,

Governor Brendan Byrne, Attorney General Grewal, and Mercer County Prosecutor Onofri. It's kinda his thing."

"Strange thing," said Rich with a smile. "So, I heard you kids are ambassadors. Tell me about that."

While we explained our jobs, T-Bone continued to stare. I was tempted to close his eyes just to make him blink. When we told Rich about our fire and safety project, he was impressed and offered to assist. That was about the exact time T-Bone nearly fainted.

"*You* want to help *us*?" he asked.

"Sure," he said. "Firefighters are born to help others. You know, I used to be a captain in the Morristown Fire Department."

"Morristown?" asked T-Bone, coming out of his stupor. "We've done reports on Morristown, twice. We love the Morristown Green, Jockey Hollow, the Ford Mansion, and Fosterfields Historic Farm! We recently went to the Schuyler-Hamilton House, too."

"Wow, you certainly know Morristown," he said with a smile. "How's your fire service report coming along, anyway?"

"Pretty good," I said. "We've visited firefighters in Trenton, Atlantic City, Vineland, and Union Township."

"And we met the president and vice presidents of the FMBA," said Wanda. "They've been really helpful."

"So, you've met Eddie, Wayne, and Tim?" asked Rich.

"You know them, too?" asked T-Bone. "Do all firefighters know each other?"

"No, we don't all know each other," he laughed. "There's over 37,000 firefighters in New Jersey's Fire Service, but I do know Eddie, Wayne, and Tim. You see, I used to be the Vice President of the FMBA."

"No way!" said T-Bone. "Although I forget what all of those letters stand for. They sure picked big and unusual words, but I do know that one of those words isn't gelatin."

"Gelatin?" he asked. "No, no it's the New Jersey Firefighters Mutual Benevolent Association."

"We kind of know what it is, but if you don't mind me asking, what exactly is it?" asked Wanda.

"I guess the easiest way to describe it is that it's an organization to protect the people who protect the people," said Rich. "They do very important things like making sure firefighters work in safe conditions…"

"Safe conditions?" T-Bone interupted. "They literally work in the opposite of safe conditions. They run into danger when everyone else is running away from danger. How is that keeping them safe? If you want to really keep them safe, you should tell them to work from home."

Rich laughed and said, "I can see how it can be confusing. But people who risk their lives for others need proper equipment and protective gear, trucks must be maintained, and then smart policies must be implemented. My office actually writes the codes and rules that departments must follow."

"Sounds like a gigantic responsibility," I said.

"It is," Rich agreed. "We oversee training, codes, preparedness, community risk reduction, and juvenile firesetters."

"That's strange," said T-Bone. "It almost sounded like you said juvenile firesetters, like kids setting fires. But that can't be right."

"That's correct," he said. "Each year, kids are burned or even die because of fires they set. Whether it's curiosity or something deeper, we want to teach kids how serious fire is, how fast it spreads, and how deadly it can be."

"I get training and community risk reduction," I said, "but what's preparedness and codes? Is that like computer coding?"

"No," Rich laughed, "but I see how you could be confused. These codes are building and safety codes. They're basically rules that we establish and enforce to keep people safe."

"So, like rules that buildings have to have EXIT signs that light up and sprinklers?" I asked.

"Exactly," he agreed. "And preparedness is how we work with lots of different agencies, like the State Police and Homeland

Security, on how to respond to major incidents. You kids weren't alive for 9/11, but it really was a nightmare for First Responders. We did, however, learn a lot from it, especially when it comes to coordination."

"We've seen the footage and learned about it in school," said Wanda.

"I remember watching a hearing where Jon Stewart, John Feal, and Luis Alvarez was testifying before Congress," said Pop. "They were begging them to provide money for the First Responders who got really sick from 9/11. It was so frustrating that they had to beg for money for heroes."

"That was definitely hard to watch," said Rich. "So many heroes responded and never knew how many chemicals were on that pile. There were literally thousands of toxins. And they went back every day, digging by hand and passing buckets of debris from two giant skyscrapers that collapsed on thousands of people. So many of our brothers and sisters were killed and so many First Responders ended up with serious illnesses."

"Were Jon, John, and Luis all firefighters?" I asked.

"No," said Rich. "John Feal is a retired construction worker and was the demolition supervisor at Ground Zero. Luis Alvarez was an NYPD Bomb Squad Detective. And, Jon Stewart is a New Jersey guy that became a very popular comedian and talk show host. He felt so strongly about certain issues that he used his platform to help draw attention to them. And, he didn't just write a check. He became an amazing activist and was right there with them, side-by-side, as they fought. So, in my book, they're all heroes."

"That definitely makes them special kinds of heroes," said Wanda. "They stepped up to help the people who, despite all of the danger, never backed down."

"Indeed," said Rich. "Now they're fighting on behalf of our military members who've been severely injured and experienced illnesses from burn pits."

"I want to make a difference like Jon Stewart, John Feal and Luis Alvarez," said T-Bone.

"It sounds like you kids are on your way," said Rich.

"Hey, kids, your order is ready," said Captain Paul. "And I see you've met my friend, Rich."

"We did," said T-Bone. "He knows my very good friends, Eddie Donnelly, Wayne Wolk, and Tim Duetsch."

That was exactly how T-Bone thought about people. If he met you once, he considered you a good friend. And if you were a stranger, he believed you were just a future friend.

"Do you ever go to Trenton?" asked T-Bone.

"That's where my office is," Rich replied. "Do you?"

"We love Trenton and deliver our reports to the State House

for the governor," said T-Bone, clearly trying to brag. "We kind of work for the governor, unofficially, that is."

"Me, too," said Rich, "but in my case officially. I'm appointed by the Governor."

"Seriously?" asked T-Bone. "We've been trying to get appointed as the Official Junior Ambassadors forever. We never met the governor, but we do know Billy in the Governor's Office."

"Billy's a great guy," said Rich. "You must be pretty important if you're on a first name basis with him."

"I guess," said T-Bone, considering what Rich had just said. "Maybe you can put a good word in for us?"

"I could," he began, "but I wonder..."

"Wonder what?" asked a curious T-Bone.

"I'm just thinking out loud, but I wonder if it would make that big of a difference. Would it change all the good work you're doing for the state and for kids all over New Jersey? And now, with the work you're doing for firefighters, too? Maybe the work you're doing is bigger than a label and you don't need three words to define you. You kids are amazing. Do you really think being elevated from unofficial to official would really matter all that much?"

T-Bone thought about it for a moment. Then he nodded and said, "Yes. Yes, it would matter very much."

Chapter Twelve

Protecting the Heroes

The next morning, I looked up Jon Stewart. Rich was right. He really was from New Jersey, he did have a popular talk show, and he did fight for First Responders. Then I read about John Feal. John Feal was working at Ground Zero when a falling steel beam landed on his foot. As a result, he had to have part of his foot amputated, yet he was denied benefits. He knew this was happening to so many other victims and he decided to do something about it. He fought to have the 9/11 Victims Compensation Fund made permanent. This was the money paid to the victims of 9/11. John Feal has fought with Jon Stewart, side-by-side, on behalf of First Responders, for decades. I was confused as to why this fund wasn't permanent in the first place. When I asked Pop, he just shook his head and told me *politics*. That answer still didn't make sense to me. Who votes against First Responders?

When I did more research on 9/11, I learned that so many New Jersey firefighters assisted their brothers and sisters in the FDNY. I read that the trains going in and out of New York City were closed, except for those bringing in First Responders. Wayne told me about the firefighters from the Trenton Fire Department that boarded trains headed to Penn Station to provide assistance. He said the train ride into New York was filled with tactical conversations and when they arrived, the station was eerily quiet and empty. When the firefighters took the escalator to the main floor, the people who were taking refuge all stood and clapped as they walked by. He said those firefighters remember that moment like it was yesterday.

I couldn't understand why heroes had to beg to be taken care of, or why people had to even consider providing for them. What was to consider? Afterall, they never hesitate, not even for a moment, when the bell rings. I learned more about Luis Alvarez, too. As an NYPD Bomb Squad Detective, he became extremely sick with cancer from working on the pile at Ground Zero. He knocked on the doors of Congress and the Senate with Jon Stewart and John Feal right up until he died. There had to be a better way, I thought. I was so angry that Luis had to spend what little time he had left begging for benefits.

Hopefully, T-Bone was right and Wanda would become a politician and make positive changes. While I was relieved that people like John Feal, Jon Stewart, and Luis Alvarez fought for First Responders, it shouldn't have been this difficult. Even though I wasn't sure if I would ever become a firefighter, I was sure about one thing. One day, I wanted to shake hands with John Feal and Jon Stewart just to thank them both.

As I continued my research, I learned all about John Feal's FealGood Foundation. They did amazing, tireless work, but it wasn't just *what* kind of assistance they were providing. It was *who* they were assisting: all emergency personnel, including but not limited to firefighters, police officers, nurses, volunteers, sanitation workers, transportation workers and construction workers, within the United States who have been injured in the course of their duties or within their everyday lives.

Their mission included educating people, elected officials and organizations on the various problems, concerns and issues faced by First Responders in their everyday duties. They were dedicated to advocating for First Responder rights as well as illuminating the serious issues they encounter.

When I first learned about all of this, I wished I had had the chance to meet Luis Alvarez and I still wanted to meet Jon Stewart and John Feal. By the time I finished my research, I didn't just want to meet them and thank them, I wanted to help them. I wasn't sure how, but I planned on getting involved and helping to protect the people that protect the people.

While I waited for Wanda and T-Bone to arrive, I watched a little bit of the Phillies game. We planned to head up to Trenton to give our reports to Billy and then we planned to stop by the Old Barracks. It was shaping up to be a good day until Wanda burst through the front door. It was strange because T-Bone always barged in, and Wanda always knocked.

"Hurry, Nicky, come with me!" she said while she tried to catch her breath. "Hurry up! Now!"

"Come where?" I asked as I jumped up and followed her. "What's happening?"

"A car accident," she said, still panting. "It's pretty bad. T-Bone's there now. He told me to get you."

"Get me?" I gasped. "Did he call 9-1-1? Is help on the way?"

"Yes, he called for help," she said as we ran faster. "But the car hit a tree. We saw the whole thing. A dog ran out and the woman swerved to avoid it."

My heart was racing, and my stomach felt sick. As we got closer, I could see the car, smashed into the tree with airbags coming through the window.

"Nick, I called 9-1-1 and gave the size-up," yelled T-Bone. "There's a female around 30, probably 40, but I don't want to insult her. And there's a little boy in the back. Cute kid, maybe 3-years-old. At least old enough to be in a forward-facing seat."

"What?" I said, wondering why he was telling me.

"Don't just stand there," he said taking off his sweatshirt. "Find me a rock and I'll wrap my sweatshirt around it and break the passenger window."

"Okay, slow down," I replied. "How do you know there's a little kid in there and how do you know if you can break a window with a rock in a sweatshirt?"

"The kid waved at me right before the crash," he said. "I have a way with kids and dogs. It's actually uncanny. Anyway, why are you asking so many questions?"

"I don't know," I yelled back, trying not panic. "I've never been a first responder before."

"Technically, you're a third responder, behind me and then behind Wanda," he corrected me.

"I don't think that's how this works," I said. "And did you try to open the doors?"

"Nick!" he yelled. "The vehicle is wrapped around a tree. Of course, the doors won't open. We're probably gonna need the jaws of life."

Before he could finish his sentence, Wanda collected herself and went over to try the door handle. It worked. The mom was crying and telling her little boy everything would be okay. The boy was screaming, and T-Bone ran over to his door.

"Is my son okay?" the woman asked repeatedly. "Is he okay?"

"Standby," said T-Bone. "Okay, I have a visual on him. He's crying pretty hard, but he looks like he's in one piece. Sounds like he's saying *wire duck, wire duck*. Someone find out what *wire duck* means. STAT!"

"Maybe he drank an energy drink and he's saying he's wired up," I guessed, now actually starting to panic.

"Why would a toddler drink an energy drink?" T-Bone snapped. "C'mon, Nick, pull yourself together!"

"He's saying fire truck," said the woman. "He must have dropped his toy fire truck. Please find it for him if you can. It might calm him down."

"Are you in pain," I asked her. "Are you hurt?"

"I think my head is bleeding," she said as she felt her forehead. "But I think I'm okay. My door is stuck."

"See!" T-Bone exclaimed. "I was right. We need the jaws of life."

"Hold on," said Wanda as she unlocked the woman's door. "Here you go, I can open it now."

We were about to pull her out when T-Bone immediately stopped us. He insisted she could have back, or neck injuries and we shouldn't move her. He said we needed to wait for the First Responders. Wanda and I stood there in shock. He was right. You shouldn't move someone unless it's too dangerous to remain where they are. It was strange watching T-Bone remain so calm during such a stressful incident. A moment later, we heard the sirens of a fire truck, ambulance, and a police car.

T-Bone explained how the accident occurred to the police and then gave his report to the fire chief. He stared at T-Bone for a moment and said, "Did you call this accident in?"

T-Bone was about to say yes, and then thought it over. "Why? Would I be in trouble if I did?"

"Actually," he said, "you wouldn't be in any trouble at all. I'm only asking because the dispatcher said the call sounded like it came from an off-duty firefighter, and I don't see anyone else here."

"I'm not an off-duty firefighter. I actually consider myself an amateur, more of an enthusiast," said T-Bone. "But if you'd like to consider me an Unofficial Junior Off-Duty Firefighter, I wouldn't mind."

"Wow, that's a lot of information," said Chief Todd. "But either way, good job. Very good job."

"Hey Nick, what do you think about that?" asked T-Bone. "My size-up sounded professional. Chief Todd said I sounded professional, and I didn't even flee. Maybe I'll end up in the fire service after all."

"Excuse me," the woman said as the EMT pushed the gurney past us. "Please stop for a second."

The EMT stopped pushing as the woman looked at T-Bone and said, "I can't thank you enough for staying with us. That was really scary. All of you, thank you so much. And thanks for finding my son's truck."

"No problem," said T-Bone as they loaded the woman and her son in the ambulance. "All in a day's work."

"A day's work?" I asked, almost out of breath. "Whose day?"

"The firefighters," he said. "And for a few minutes, I knew what it felt like to be one of them. Minus the cool uniform and the fire truck. But you know what I mean."

"I have to hand it to you," said Wanda. "You were cool as a cucumber. That was pretty impressive."

T-Bone smiled and turned redder than the fire truck.

By the time we returned to my house, Pop had pulled up and we couldn't wait to tell him what had happened. He laughed and told T-Bone he might have just caught the firefighting bug. T-Bone admitted that it was a rush to help someone in trouble.

"So, we're off to the Old Barracks and the State House?" Pop asked, confirming our short itinerary.

"Yup, but I was wondering if we could make one other stop in Trenton," I said.

"Sure," he said with a wink. "I'm taking your grandmother to Marsilio's Kitchen tonight, but we should have plenty of time."

"You sure never sit still, do you?" said T-Bone.

"Why should I?" said Pop with a laugh. "Too many great things to see and do."

We headed to the State House first and saw two familiar faces talking to Billy. It was the Rich Mikutsky the State Fire Marshall and Eddie Donnelly the FMBA President. They immediately recognized us and opened the glass door.

"Well, look who it is," said Eddie. "How are New Jersey's finest tour guides doing today?"

"Actually, we're ambassadors," said T-Bone.

"I know," said Eddie. "I'm just teasing you."

"But you'll never guess what happened," T-Bone continued.

"I give up," said Rich.

"You didn't even try," said T-Bone. "You're supposed to guess."

"I'm pretty sure you said that I'll never guess what happened, so I'm taking your word for it," he said and smiled at the rest of us.

"Good point, you'd probably never guess," said T-Bone. "I caught my first run, arrived on scene, called dispatch, and did a size up."

"Hold on," said Eddie. "Aren't you the chili, dalmatians, and video games guy? The hammocks, bagpipes, and cotton candy guy? You're that guy, right?"

"Used to be," said T-Bone. "But you really opened my eyes."

"What happened?" asked Rich.

"Thanks to Eddie, all of the firefighters we met in Trenton, Vineland, Atlantic City, and Union Township, I get it," said T-Bone. "I finally get it."

"Those must have been some visits," said Eddie, "because you sound like you already went through the fire academy."

"Not yet," said T-Bone, "but helping that mother and her son was exhilarating."

"You, my friend," said Rich, "have caught the firefighting bug."

"Is that how most people get started?" I asked. "Did you catch the bug?"

"My neighbors were volunteer firefighters and I thought it was so cool," said Rich. "As soon as I turned 18 years old, I joined the local fire house as a volunteer. After four years, I took the fire test, and then got hired."

"Maybe I'll do that," said T-Bone. "How old do you have to be to get started? Is this a 12 and up type of thing?"

"It's a fire academy," Eddie laughed. "Not a summer camp. Candidates need to be over 18-years-old."

"That's fair," said T-Bone. "Plus, I'll be busy with high school for the next four years. But, one question, can you say you're a firefighter when you're in the academy?"

"Sure," said Rich, "but your first year is your probationary year."

"Oh, I get it," said T-Bone. "That's when you have to be on your best behavior."

"We actually prefer firefighters to be on their best behavior throughout their career," said Rich. "Probationary firefighters, or probies, have extra mentoring and supervision while they learn on the job."

"That's a good idea," said Wanda. "Experience is the best teacher."

"You've got that right," said Rich. "And thanks for everything you're doing. Anyone or anything that works to keep people and First Responders safe is alright with me."

"Agreed," said Eddie. "You're all doing fine work, including you, T-Bone."

"Hey, you finally got my name right," said T-Bone.

"I knew it all along,"Eddie said with a smile.

"So, we're heading in to meet with the Governor," said Rich. "You kids keep up the good work."

"Put in a good word for us," T-Bone said as they walked away.

We spoke to Billy and shared everything we learned. He was impressed that we were able to manage so many fire tips and promised to have them on the website that week. We walked out of the state house, made a right and turned at the corner of Thomas Edison State University.

The Old Barracks Museum was right down the street. As we got closer, it smelled amazing. I couldn't put my finger on it at first, but it was fantastic. Then I realized it was the warm aroma of fresh bread. We walked through the front gate and were greeted by Asher and Daryian. They explained that today was a bread day and then took us around back to the new historic brick oven. It was huge and they told us they could bake one hundred loaves of bread at a time.

As we approached the oven, Michelle and Rebecca were taking loaves out and placing them on cooling racks. "Would you like some warm bread with honey butter?" asked Michelle.

The last time I had honey butter on warm bread was at Legends Pizza in Burlington and it was amazing. We all said yes. It was so amazing that we didn't notice David, under the pavilion, doing colonial woodworking. We walked up and he showed us the tools he was using and explained each one. Interestingly, he had to make the tools before he could do the work. I forgot they didn't have hardware stores to buy power tools like we do.

Asher then invited us into the Officer's House, and we went upstairs to the tailor shop where master tailor, David sewed all of the staff's attire. From there we met his real brother, Damian, the expert shoemaker, who was making shoes by hand. I didn't even think that was possible. I thought that was only in fairy tales, but he made all of the shoes for the staff. We walked through the medical room and the bunk rooms until we reached the gift shop. I wanted to go outside and get more bread, but I didn't want to be rude. Lauren and Vikki must have read my mind because they came in with pre-buttered slices of warm bread. Still not wanting to be rude, I took six, or seven slices. It might have been twelve. It was so good, I lost count.

Once inside the gift shop we met up with Richard, James, and Colleen. "Looks like the gang's all here," said T-Bone.

"Well, word spreads quick when New Jersey's ambassadors show up," said Richard. "And you picked a great day."

"We could smell the bread at the State House," said Wanda. "That aroma is sure to bring a crowd of state workers over for some fresh loaves."

I loved the whole new living history vibe at the Old Barracks. Besides the tours, visitors could now watch colonial trades like shoemaking, tailoring, woodworking, and baking. There were so many changes we decided to keep coming back.

We stayed and talked for a moment and then told them that we were on our way to Rivera School for the Trenton Youth Wrestling Beat the Streets event. They had heard great things about the program and said we would really enjoy it.

They were right. From the moment we walked in, you could feel the excitement. There were three giant mats and a medley of sights, sounds, and smells. I didn't know a lot about wrestling, but this looked incredible. We saw Dave Leonardis standing with a group of wrestlers and as we got closer, we realized there were boys and girls in the group.

"Hey Dave," said T-Bone. "We're here."

"Hey, kids, great to see you," said Dave. "Come meet some of our amazing wrestlers."

We said hello to everyone and wished all of them luck. I didn't exactly know how wrestling matches worked, but I was extremely excited.

The clinic began and the Trenton wrestlers were really talented. This was nothing like the chair-breaking wrestling matches I used to watch with my dad. This was all about skill and strategy. This sport clearly required a lot of discipline and patience. Trenton's wrestlers were really fantastic.

"Hey, kids," said a voice from behind us.

"Hi Dr. McLaughlin," said T-Bone. "This is really awesome."

"I'm glad you're enjoying it," he said. "There's always so much energy here."

"And this guy knows about energy," said Dave as he walked up to our group. "Dr. McLaughlin has more energy than anyone."

"This is really incredible," said Wanda. "How did this program get started?"

"Well, I was a wrestler and my kids were wrestlers," said Dr. McLaughlin. "When they grew up, I missed it. Wrestling teaches so many life lessons. So, I reached out to the Bethea family in Trenton. Then with Dave, we started building this program."

"How did you find so many kids?" I asked.

"See all of the kids we have now?" asked Dave.

"Yup," said T-Bone.

"We didn't start out this big," he laughed. "We started with a small group and now we're up to 160 kids. The College of New Jersey has been very supportive, and we also work closely with Rider University, Princeton University, and Rutgers University."

"Wow, we were just at The College of New Jersey," I said. "That's so cool that the colleges are involved."

"It sure is," said Dave. "I used to teach there, so I'm very proud of their involvement. In fact, a number of TCNJ wrestlers help coach. Thanks to this program, some of our wrestlers are elite athletes."

"What's the wrestling season look like?" asked Wanda.

"Well, we have this clinic in the summer each year and then our season runs from November through February," said Dr. McLaughlin. "We're in the Delaware River League with 25 other teams. We host the tournaments here on Saturdays and the kids practice Monday through Friday."

"Practice must be really fun," said T-Bone.

"It's fun, but it's also hard work," said Dr. McLaughlin. "This is a scholar athlete program, so the emphasis is as much on academics and personal responsibility as it is on wrestling."

"I like that idea," said T-Bone. "It's like eating your vegetables before you can eat dessert."

"Well, we offer healthy snacks and the cooler's always open," said Dave.

"Just make sure the seagulls aren't around when you open it up," said T-Bone. "They're thieves."

"Duly noted," said Dave. "We also provide books, tutoring, and a good workout."

"The kids must really love it," said Wanda.

"They do," said Dr. Mclaughlin, "but it's much bigger than that. We provide kids with an alternative to the streets. And with wrestling, kids can also work out their aggression in a safe environment. It's only you on the mat, so you have to dig deep."

"I never thought about the aggression aspect, but it makes sense," I said.

"And our training camp," said Dave, "it teaches life lessons and how wrestling relates to life. Dr. McLaughlin even brought in Olympic Gold Medalists to speak to our kids."

This was exactly what Pastor Taylor's Capital City Community Coalition was all about, people coming together for the greater good. For Trenton Youth Wrestling, a Special Investigator from the Attorney General's Office and a Neurosurgeon came together with the Bethea family to make such a difference. Maybe that was the key to doing great things – finding other people to work with, pooling resources, and sharing the load.

We stayed for a while, had a snack with the kids, and then had a chance to hear how much they loved it. They were so passionate about wrestling and about the program. This was definitely making a difference in their lives. As we were leaving, we promised to return when the season started and even volunteered to help. We knew nothing about wrestling, but we could help tutor and we could definitely root for them.

A few days later, just as my mom was putting dinner on the table, T-Bone came strolling into the kitchen.

"Is the doorbell broken?" asked my dad sarcastically.

"Wouldn't know," said T-Bone as he grabbed a corn-on-the-cob. "I don't think I've ever used it."

"I know," my dad sighed. "I know."

A moment later, the doorbell did ring and this time it was Wanda. Before she could even sit down, the doorbell rang again. My mom answered the door and then called for us. There was a woman and a little boy standing there.

"Kids, this is Wanda Russo," said my mom. "The woman that you helped from the car accident."

"Hi kids, I just wanted to come by and thank you for all of your help," she said. "That was such an awful day. A dog ran in front of my car, and when I tried not to hit it, I ending up sliding into the tree."

"How are you feeling?" asked my dad.

"Still a little sore," she said, "but mostly grateful. That accident could have been a lot worse. Especially having my little Tommy in the car with me."

"Wait, what?" said T-Bone. "Your son's name is Tommy Russo? That's almost my name. I'm Tommy Rizzo."

"Yes, he's named after my husband, Tom, although we usually just call my husband, T," she said.

"Wait, your name is Wanda, and you married a man named Tom? Tom Russo?" T-Bone gasped.

"Yes, I did," she said. "Why?"

"Hold on," said T-Bone, "you just said they call your husband T? Is that, by any chance, short for T-Bone?"

"No," she laughed. "It's short for Tom. I thought that was pretty obvious."

"Can I ask you another question?" said T-Bone. "Did you and Tom meet in elementary school and decide to go to the senior prom together before high school even started?"

"We did meet in high school," she said, rather confused by the whole conversation. "I think he asked me to go a couple of months before the prom. Sorry, it's been a while. Anyway, I just wanted to stop by and thank you."

By that point, T-Bone had stopped listening. While Wanda Russo told us about how little Tommy kept calling us heroes, all T-Bone heard was that a Wanda married a Tommy.

"I was wondering" said T-Bone. "What's your husband's job?"

"He's a firefighter," she said.

"I'm sorry, but did you, Wanda, say that your husband, Tommy, who also goes by T, is a firefighter?" asked T-Bone.

"Yes, and boy was he a wreck when he got the call about our accident," she replied. "He responds to emergencies so often, but it's very different when it's your own family."

T-Bone's face lit up as though all of this was a giant sign from the universe. He looked at Wanda Russo like she was proof that he could one day marry our friend, Wanda, and even become a firefighter. He believed there was a reason their paths crossed. Right now, T-Bone was as hopeful as he had ever been, maybe even more hopeful. And maybe Rich was right, too. Perhaps T-Bone did catch the firefighting bug.

There was absolutely no way to know what the future would look like. Since some really good jobs, like trades, didn't require a degree, we didn't even know if we were all going to college. And if we all did attend college, we had no idea where we would go. I figured it wasn't impossible that we could all live T-Bone's dream and attend The College of New Jersey while sharing an apartment together in Campus Town. Or, we could be scattered across the country. And, because we had no idea what we wanted to be when we grew up, there was no possible way to know where we would eventually work.

At times, it seemed pretty overwhelming. When they gave us this assignment, I assumed this must be something we should already know. Luckily, Pop told us that the uncertainty was what made these years so exciting. Our lives were filled with so much opportunity and so many choices. He expected that we would all explore, learn, and grow as we found our path. I wasn't sure why he was so confident in us, but he told us that it had been his pleasure to watch us grow for last several years.

As exciting as all of this uncharted territory was, it did present a problem. I still had to complete my summer assignment and write an essay about what I wanted to be when I grew up. After speaking to Pop, I considered writing something like this:

At this time, professionally speaking, I have no idea what I'd like to be when I grow up. Right now, my life is wide open and filled with endless opportunities. Each day and each experience pushes me closer to where I'll end up, but where that is...I have no idea. If my life was a book, I couldn't sneak ahead to read the last chapter because it hasn't been written yet. And to be honest, I'm kind of happy not knowing.

I wasn't sure if my answer would be acceptable, but it was definitely the truth. There were very few things I knew for certain and where our lives would end up was definitely not one of them.

In fact, there was only one thing that I was truly certain about. T-Bone was going to be a very, very busy guy. He now had roughly three years to convince Wanda to go to the Junior Prom.

The End

Safety Tips From

New Jersey's Bravest

Call 9-1-1.

Know Your Location.

Establish a Meeting Place.

Get low and go.

Never Go Back Inside.

Never Play With Matches.

Don't Overload Extension Cords.

Never Hide.

Always make sure your campfire is completely extinguished and follow all rules.

Install smoke and
carbon monoxide detectors.

Make sure all detectors
have working batteries.

Wear a seatbelt.

Never stay in a hot car.

Never distract the driver.

Never swim alone.

Never go near downed wires.

Never walk on train tracks.